MOUNTAIN IMPACT

ALSO BY J.R. PACE

Mont Blanc Rescue Series

Book 1: Mountain Struggle

Book 2: Mountain Impact

Book 3: Mountain Trial

Book 4: Mountain Shadow

Book 5: Mountain Deadpoint

**

Sharp's Cove Series

Book 1: One Night Years Ago

Book 2: Two Favors Repaid

Book 3: Three Times Ablaze

**

Grim Reapers Series

Book 1: Storme's Match

Book 2: Sawyer's Mistake

Book 3: Prado's Choice

**

Standalone Novella

Cold and Bitter Snow

MOUNTAIN IMPACT

MONT BLANC RESCUE BOOK 2

J.R. PACE

Mountain Impact

Published by J.R. Pace

Copyright 2021 by J.R. Pace

Cover design by Maria Spada

ISBN: 978-84-09-35373-6

Note to readers: This book contains adult scenes and language, and is intended for adult readers.

You are not in the mountains.
The mountains are in you.

-- John Muir

Drake

Drake Jacobs tightened his hold on the handlebars. Until now, he'd been coursing gently down the forest trail, but he'd now reached the spot where the trail became more technical—and a lot more fun.

He stood on the pedals, holding his hips back and his head up as he thundered down the slope. Standing at six-four and over two hundred and forty pounds, most of it muscle, Drake was a big man, but he wasn't worried about his bike. He'd had it upgraded to cope with what the local bike store referred to as a *heavy-duty load*.

This was Drake's favorite part of mountain biking,

that overwhelming feeling of freedom that hit as he sped down after a hard climb.

He rode hard but kept his index fingers on the break levers in case any hikers or dogs suddenly appeared—both, he knew from painful experience, could come out of nowhere and, while he didn't mind hitting the ground, he wasn't about to risk hitting anybody else.

His front wheel hit a small rock, threatening to send him to the ground. Drake corrected—he managed to stay on the bike, but miscalculated and grazed his arm against a nearby tree, giving himself a bark tattoo.

He hissed in pain, but didn't stop.

He'd made a bet with himself that he could make the run in two hours, and that wouldn't happen if he stopped to admire the view. But then again, it was his day off—and it's not like he had anybody waiting for him back at home.

Something glinted on the ground before him—he was moving too fast to tell with certainty, but he was pretty sure what it was. He braked hard and got off his bike, backtracking a few steps to where the shiny object lay—indeed, it was an energy gel wrapper. He picked it up and held it in his hand for a moment. There was nothing he hated more than people who dropped litter on the trails—or anywhere in the mountains.

He spared an uncharitable thought for the asshole who'd dropped the plastic wrapper, knowing it wasn't going to decompose for oh, say, six or seven hundred years.

Would it have killed them to stick it back in their pack until they could drop it in a trash can?

Drake dug in his own pack for the small bag he always carried to keep his trash in. He allowed himself a final uncharitable thought for the idiots who thought they needed an energy gel as soon as they stepped out of their front door. If they'd bothered to research the topic at all, they'd know it takes a person a long while to need—

An unfamiliar hissing sound from above had Drake raising his head in alarm. The only thing above him was the Brévent cable car, and there was no reason for that sound, unless—Drake stared, open-mouthed, as a cabin plunged into the air, crashing onto the ground. In an instant, it disappeared from sight, but he could hear it tearing down trees as it tumbled down the mountain.

Fuck.

It was a scene right out of one of his nightmares.

In his hand, Drake still grasped the small trash bag that might just have saved his life, by delaying his descent those extra minutes.

He dumped it unceremoniously into his backpack and fished for his cell phone, praying it was properly charged. He hadn't been expecting to speak with anyone today. He dialed the local emergency number, one of only three numbers he knew by heart.

"I need help," he began, and was cut off immediately by a professional-sounding female voice.

"Sir, what's your emergency?"

"Drake Jacobs here, with the PGHM," he said, speaking loudly over the sound of screeching metal. Holding the phone to his ear, he started running down the slope.

"Sir, what's your emergency?" the operator repeated stonily.

"Please look me up. Drake Jacobs," he begged, spelling out his last name. His foot hit a rock, and he almost stumbled to the ground, barely managing to right himself while keeping the phone to his ear. "I'm below the Brévent cable car. There's been an accident. I need you to put me through to Colonel Pelegrin."

Drake jumped over an overturned log, following the destruction the cabin had left behind it as it slammed into the trees. Up in the air it might have seemed small, but the twelve-person cabin was the size of a mini bus—there was no mistaking the path it'd taken.

When she didn't reply, Drake kept going.

"One of the cabins just crashed into the trees and went down the mountain. I'm running towards it now," he panted.

"What did you say your name was?"

"Drake Jacobs," Drake said in a clipped voice.

"Please hold. I'm patching you in with the colonel," the voice said.

"Jacobs? Is that you?"

Drake stumbled again, this time ending up on his knees on the velvet green forest floor. He put his palm to the ground to steady himself.

"Colonel Pelegrin, the Brévent cable car is down. I repeat, one of the cabins just crashed into the forest."

"How far away from Plan Praz are you?" the colonel asked.

Drake knew what the man was asking—the cable car connected Plan Praz and Le Brévent. At different points in the journey, the cable car could fly anywhere between thirty and two hundred feet off the ground. There was a big difference between those two figures in terms of the likelihood of finding survivors.

Drake didn't get the chance to answer. In the distance, he could see the cabin. It was lying on its side, crumpled but still recognizable.

Cold sweat broke on his forehead.

Not again. Not this.

Drake's mind flashed back to another cable car accident years earlier. Different time, different place, different cable car. The familiar phantom pain in his leg struck again—he'd been feeling it less and less in recent years, but it was like an old, never-forgotten friend.

Of course you're being triggered.

A cable car fell just in front of you.

He clenched his hands into fists. He couldn't let himself slip into a full-blown panic attack—not when so much depended on him.

A screamed ripped the air—a high, pained sound that brought Drake back from his stupor.

"There's at least one person inside. I have to go, Colonel. I'm sending the exact location of the crash site."

"Be careful, Jacobs," Colonel Pelegrin said, cutting the connection.

With shaking hands, Drake shared his location. He trusted the colonel to get it to the right people—including his team.

The scream came again. Drake approached the wreck from the top side. The cabin was balanced precariously on a ledge—several large trees had stopped its fall for now, but it could go off again any second.

He, for one, didn't want to be anywhere nearby when that happened.

Isolde

Dr. Isolde Durant's colleagues were looking at her like she'd just sprouted a set of antennae on her forehead, rather than simply turned up at a crash site wearing a pair of jeans and sneakers.

Yes, I have days off, and sometimes I choose to wear jeans.

She shouldn't have been surprised—most of the time the *gendarmes* only saw her in the office, where she was always wearing one of her professional, dark pant suits and a pair of black, low-heeled pumps.

Isolde purposefully didn't hang out with people outside of work—it's not that she was antisocial, but rather that her job as a police psychologist required impartiality, of the kind that was impossible to show once you'd been out sharing beers and laughs with someone.

Or once you'd been to bed with someone.

She shook her head to rid herself of the troublesome memory. That was *not* going to happen again.

Isolde had started working with the Chamonix police force right after finishing her PhD in Police & Public Safety Psychology seven years earlier. Policing was a dangerous, high-stress career anywhere, one where mental health issues were as common, if not more common, than physical ailments. But out here in the mountains, in one of the busiest mountain rescue services in the world, Isolde knew her job offering therapy, counseling, and stress management techniques to the brave men and women who kept the mountains safe was essential.

Unlike other police psychologists, who still advocated old-fashioned counseling approaches, Isolde didn't like to get people together in groups to discuss their feelings—everything she did was designed to avoid pathologizing normal responses to trauma.

It was her dream that some of the techniques they were trying out here would, over the next years, be implemented in other progressive police departments around the world, and lead to an improvement in officers' mental and emotional health.

Isolde was rarely out on the field, however—most of the time she worked from her office, on the top floor of the Chamonix police station. It was only once in a while that a critical accident or rescue scene was considered such high risk that she got called in on-site to offer immediate support to first responders.

A kind of psychological first aid.

So here she was, on a Sunday morning, staring at the crumpled remains of a cable car. She looked on, horrified, but unable to look away.

Nobody could have survived this.

Two firefighters stood nearby, spraying something at the remains.

"Did anybody survive?" she asked the uniformed officers standing next to her, dreading the answer. The young man and woman looked up at her.

"There were only two men on board, and they're both alive. The cabin was held up by those trees up there for a minute, before dropping again and crashing all the way down here. They were rescued just before the second drop."

Isolde looked to where they were pointing. She could see what was left of the trees that must have held it in place before it went off the ledge.

My God.

"They're okay?"

The officer nodded. "They've been taken to the hospital with fractures, but they were both conscious and speaking—a miracle, if you ask me, after falling thirty feet and then tumbling down the mountain. They were lucky to get out before that last fall—that's the one that pulverized the cable car."

"I'd like to speak to the first responders," she said, amazed that they'd been able to get to the men that quickly.

"He was here just a few minutes ago."

"Check behind those trees. That's where I last saw him," the young woman said.

"*He?*" Isolde asked. "There's only one first responder?"

"Yes. Apparently, he was mountain biking in the area. He was lucky not to be squashed like a bug by the falling cabin. He's one of the PGHM—big guy, with brown hair and gray eyes," the uniform supplied helpfully.

Isolde's heart sank at the description.

Drake Jacobs.

She inhaled slowly.

It can't be him.

That description could fit several men.

It doesn't have to be him.

But she knew she was kidding herself.

"Thank you," Isolde said, rubbing her palms along the side of her jeans.

Isolde didn't consider herself a coward, but she suddenly found herself hoping that Drake had left the scene already. If so, she'd catch up with him the following morning in the office. It'd be easier to speak with him on her turf, rather than out here.

A moment later, those cowardly thoughts were cut off as Drake emerged from the trees, looking even taller and broader than she remembered. Larger than life. He was wearing shorts, which surprised her, until she remembered he'd been mountain biking. There was no sign of his bike.

Drake's hand froze on his mouth as he saw her. He straightened up and dropped it slowly, his icy gray eyes defiant. She didn't need any of her degrees to tell her that he'd gone behind those trees to throw up.

"Are you okay?" she asked. There was no need to introduce herself to him. He knew exactly who she was and why she was here. The two of them had lived through this before, albeit many years earlier.

Before she could help herself, her eyes went down to his right calf. Though it'd healed in the close to six years since she'd last seen the injury, it was still gruesome to look at. The scar started just below the knee and worked its way down ten inches of his leg before tapering to smooth flesh. It was a messy scar, jagged in some areas and bulging in others, the kind no surgeon would ever be proud of.

He caught her looking and scowled at her.

"What do you think? Not as neat as you expected?"

I'm amazed you can stand, let alone do what you do.

Drake took a step towards her, and Isolde suddenly felt very small. Which was interesting, because *small* was not an adjective she'd ever associated with herself. At five-six, she might be average height for a woman, but she'd always been solid—of course, most people weren't six-four, either, or built like a brick shithouse.

"I'm sorry about what happened, Drake," she said, suddenly needing to clear the air between them. If anything, his eyes got even colder—he knew she wasn't talking about what had happened today.

"You're *sorry*?" he asked tightly. "I shared things with you. And you took that information and used it to almost ruin my career."

She nodded. "I'm sorry you took it that way. My report wasn't meant—"

"There's nothing I want to say to you about what happened six years ago, Dr. Durant," he said. "You're here to talk about what happened today, right? So let's do it."

The sight of his scar and the smell of whatever the firefighter had been spraying played on her mind, threatening to bring her back to that other crash site years ago.

Isolde made a fist, curling her nails into her palms, hoping the pain would steady her, but her muscles were barely responding. Something squeezed her chest—hard—as the forest closed in on her, cold and oppressive.

Isolde knew dozens of techniques to help stop panic attacks—hell, she *taught* them—but suddenly couldn't bring any of them to mind.

I can't breathe.

I need to get out of here.

"We could speak tomorrow," she said, her voice tinny to her own ears.

"No time like the present," he replied, a sour smile playing on his full lips. He took a step forward, his cold gray eyes fixed on hers.

Isolde took an unconscious step backwards.

2

Drake

Drake stared at Isolde, waiting for her to make some witty comeback—the psychologist was smart as a whip. It was one of the things he'd liked about her all those years ago—one of many things, if he was honest with himself.

He admired her legs in those tight jeans she was wearing—he had to admit, they did amazing things for her curves. It was difficult to believe, but Isolde was even more beautiful now than she'd been when they'd met six years earlier. Still curvy and soft in all the right places, but somehow more grown up now. Her eyes were the color of pure honey, a dramatic contrast against her dark hair—some strands were tied back, as usual, to keep it out of her eyes, while the rest fell loose over her shoulders. One strand had gotten free and was falling over her eyes.

He was close enough to smell her feminine perfume. Close enough that he could almost reach out and pull that rebel strand out of her eyes. Drake shook himself. He had no business looking at her like that.

Remember what she did.

"Shall we get started? Do you want to see the cabin?"

When she didn't reply to his taunt, he stared at her more closely.

Is she paler than she was just a minute ago?

Her skin had gone sallow, her lips bleached to an almost blue tone. Her small hands were clenched into fists—her chest heaved and her whole body shook as she struggled to take in her next breath.

All of Drake's righteous anger disappeared as he realized what he was looking at.

Jesus, she's being triggered.

And you're the asshole making it worse.

"Isolde?" he asked, hating the way his voice sounded so gruff when he spoke to her. "Isolde," he repeated firmly.

She raised her eyes towards him—the pupils dilated so the entire center of her eye looked black, with only a thin honey-colored ring at the edges. But at least she was reacting to his voice.

"I think I'm going to—"

Pass out? Throw up?

Drake placed one hand gently on Isolde's back and led her to the trees he'd just walked out of, ready to pick her up if she fell. He avoided the particular tree where he'd stopped to retch a few minutes earlier and guided her to a nearby one. As soon as they were out of sight, he placed his hands under her armpits, gently encouraging her down into a sitting position.

She felt solid in his arms, real—he tried not to think about how close her breasts were to his hands.

"Sit down, Isolde, before you fall."

"I can't, somebody will—"

Her eyes, as she looked up at him, were panicked.

He understood her reserve.

"There's nobody here, Isolde. Just us," he said as gently as he could. "There, put your head between your knees—that's great. Now try to breathe. Slow and deep."

He moved back to give her space and waited, clenching his fists, as she struggled to get air into and out of her lungs. He had half a mind to go find Jens, their team's doctor, who was somewhere around.

What the hell do you know about anxiety?

She might need more support than you're able to provide.

Isolde looked up and shook her head softly—she'd always had an uncanny ability to read his mind.

Finally, her breaths slowed down enough that Drake thought she might be able to hear to his words.

"It's not the same as last time," he said quietly.

She raised her head from between her knees. "*Quoi?*"

"I said, it's not the same as last time. The two men were alive and conscious when I got them out. One hurt his leg, the other one hurt his shoulder. They're fine—or at least, Jens thinks they'll both make a full recovery."

"How did you—"

"I got lucky," he said, not wanting to get into the details of how he'd only just managed to drag the second man out when the cabin went off the ledge and rolled another fifty feet further down the mountain. Knowing that wouldn't make Isolde feel safer—and that's what she needed, to feel safer, more in control.

"It's not like last time," she repeated, like a mantra. "It's not like last time."

Something clenched inside Drake's chest.

So arrogant.

Why did I assume I was the only one whose life changed that day?

3

Isolde

I solde hit the snooze button for the third time and placed a pillow over her head to protect herself from the light streaming in through her bedroom window—she'd once again forgotten to close the blinds. Sighing, she finally turned over and sat up in bed.

She'd tossed and turned half the night, trapped in a series of nightmares of her own making. The forest had figured prominently in all of them. There'd been people trapped inside the trees at the edge of a trail— straining to get out, like animals in a cage. Isolde had hovered, sometimes over the trees, sometimes on the trail, her body moving heavily, as if wading through molasses.

She couldn't even blame the nightmares on the heat. Late summer had given way to early fall, that magical time of year when the Chamonix Valley's palette went from bright green to dusty orange ombré. It was normally Isolde's favorite time of year. She wasn't a big skier, so the entire fall season, before the snow and the hordes of winter visitors arrived, suited her just fine.

But no, one didn't need to be Freud to interpret her dreams—after yesterday's events, she knew exactly where her nightmares were coming from. Instead of doing her job, she'd let herself fall prey to a panic attack. And it'd been Drake Jacobs, of all people, who'd had to step in to help her. She bit her lower lip reflexively.

How am I going to outlive the embarrassment?

Isolde made her way to the bathroom in her black, lacy nightgown. It was the kind of outfit most women wore to please their partners, but Isolde wore it to please herself. She wasn't seeing anyone at the moment, but she loved beautiful lingerie and night-clothes—it didn't matter to her if nobody ever else got to see them. *She* liked wearing them, and didn't see any reason not to pamper herself.

She turned the overhead bathroom light on, then wished she hadn't as she caught sight of her face in the mirror. She looked exactly like what she felt like.

Puffy, frumpy, and exhausted.

Make-up might fix some of those issues.

Probably not all.

She took off her nightgown and dropped it in the laundry hamper sitting in a corner of her bathroom, then stepped into her large walk-in shower. The shower was enormous—it took up half of the bathroom, and that was after she'd renovated the bathroom and made it bigger, taking over part of the spare bedroom to do so.

She'd had to fight the architect every step of the way during her apartment's renovation a couple years earlier—the man simply refused to believe that a woman in her early thirties wouldn't be saving that second bedroom for her future family. But Isolde had been adamant. She was an independent, professional woman who knew what she wanted—and what she'd wanted was a large master suite, with an ample walk-in closet and a luxurious bathroom.

To complete the renovation, she'd closed off the small terrace off the living room and turned it into a home office. That way, she could work from home while staring at Mont Blanc and the surrounding peaks. It was a view that never failed to take her breath away.

The architect had balked at her requests but had done everything she asked—and finally, even he'd had to admit, the end result was fantastic.

Isolde turned the rainfall shower on. She didn't need to fiddle with the temperature knob, as it was always adjusted to almost-too-hot, just the way she liked it. She scrubbed her body briskly. She usually didn't pay much attention to her body—it worked well, allowed her to do everything she wanted to do, and that was usually enough for her. If her stomach was too flabby, her breasts too soft, or her thighs too large—that was a secret between her and the bathroom mirror.

She finished her shower and grabbed one of the large towels hanging from a hook right outside the shower door, wrapping herself tightly inside.

Next, she lathered herself in her favorite bergamot-scented body cream. From the time she was a little girl, her mother had drilled into her the importance of using body moisturizer to keep her skin smooth. As a child she'd hated it, gone to great lengths to avoid the process, but over time it'd become second nature to her.

She checked the time on her phone—still doing okay, but she had to get moving or she wouldn't have time to grab a cup of coffee on her way to the office.

And that would be a very bad thing.

She put on a supposedly skin-colored balcony bra —not that its pinkish shade looked much like her own skin, which had always been pale with golden undertones—hooking it behind her back in an easy, practiced move and hefting her breasts to get them to sit in the right place. After rummaging in her drawer for a while, she finally pulled out the matching panties.

Next, she picked a freshly dry-cleaned black pant suit out of her closet. There were five others hanging beside it, all very similar in fit and style. That didn't bother her in the least. The tailored pants and jacket, which combined the structure of tailoring with a bit of added stretch for her ample curves, worked for her body shape.

In winter she might pair the suit with a sleek turtleneck but, for now, she chose a cream-colored boat neck blouse that fell cleanly to her hips.

It might not be an adventurous style but she'd read somewhere that comfort created confidence, and the saying certainly seemed to be true for her.

She walked back towards her bathroom, glad to see her skin no longer looked as puffy. Her make-up routine, consisting of under-eye concealer, a hydrating foundation, light blush, mascara and a lip-colored lip gloss, took all of sixty seconds.

Armed in her professional garb, she felt better— she might not be looking forward to the day ahead, but she was now ready to face it, at least.

She finally allowed herself to think of the name that'd been hovering in the back of her mind since she first opened her eyes.

Drake Jacobs.

She was going to have to see him again, to discuss yesterday's incident. Of course, she shouldn't be the one to work with him. Their history together was not conducive to him opening up to her—and neither was her obvious, unfortunate, and lasting attraction to the man. But her colleague, François Junot, the only other psychologist in the Chamonix police, was on holiday in the south, and this wasn't the kind of thing that could wait until he got back.

Drake

Though it was barely eight a.m., the door to Isolde's office was open. Drake knew she usually came in early, so it didn't surprise him to find her sitting at her desk already.

He approached the door, rapping his knuckles sharply against the wood. Her name—Isolde—came so easily to his lips, he had to force himself to utter a more formal, "*Bonjour*, Dr Durant," instead.

He often spoke in French with her. The members of Drake's search and rescue team all came from different places, so it was only with Kat, their pilot, and sometimes with Damien, that Drake got to speak in French. The rest of the time, they worked in English. Both languages worked for Drake, even if he still got ribbed sometimes for his purportedly sing-songy Quebecois accent.

Once upon a time, Isolde used to love my accent.

He shook the memory away. He couldn't keep thinking about their brief affair. It had ended, and he needed to stop thinking about her like that.

"Isolde, please," she said automatically, standing up to greet him.

As she did so, Drake took the chance to look at her, trying not to be obvious about it. She was once again dressed in one of her dark, professional pant suits, this time paired with a cream-colored blouse that made her honey-colored eyes stand out. He kept his face neutral but allowed himself a moment of amusement—she probably thought the outfit hid her curves.

As if.

She looked better today than she had in the forest—more like herself, more in control. He knew how important that was to her—just like he knew what she looked like when she lost that control. His cock strained against his technical trousers at the thought and he fought the urge to rearrange himself—because, despite how he behaved himself whenever he was with her, he wasn't a complete asshole. And because offending her was the last thing he wanted to do.

To prevent her from noticing, he sat down on the chair opposite her desk and leaned back casually, crossing an ankle over his other knee.

"So, what now, do we follow the Critical Incident Stress Management system?"

Her eyebrows shot up in surprise. She probably hadn't imagined he'd remember the conversations they'd had about her work, but Drake remembered most things about their time together.

Isolde faltered for a moment. "I ... I'd rather just have a conversation together. I'm not looking for a formal debrief, I just want to know how you're feeling."

Drake watched as she sat back behind her desk. Her lower body disappeared, but the view of her breasts straining against that conservative blouse was still pretty fantastic. He forced himself to raise his eyes to her face.

Keep them up there, asshole.

"Okay," he said gamely.

"How are you feeling, Drake?"

"I feel ... I feel like you should clear me so I can get back to work."

She pursed her lips and he couldn't help but stare at her mouth. He liked that her lips looked bare.

So fucking kissable.

"Drake?"

He realized he'd missed her last words.

"I said that's not what you feel. That's what you want," she repeated.

Touché.

"Okay. I would like you to clear me, Isolde. Please."

She clasped her hands in front of her for a moment. "We're going to have to talk first."

"Sure," he said. "How are you feeling, Doc?"

The nickname came naturally to him—it's what he used to call her. The first time he'd used it, they'd been in bed together.

Her eyes narrowed.

Clearly, she remembers as well.

Did she also remember how just a few weeks later she'd handed in her report to his superiors, stating that Drake was having trouble processing the cable car crash and that, independently of how his leg healed, he was going to need more time before getting back to work?

"Let's talk about how *you're* feeling, Drake. You saved two people yesterday."

"But I let *her* die. Isn't that what you're thinking?"

Isolde didn't ask who he was talking about. She knew perfectly well that Drake was talking about the crash that took place six years earlier—a smaller cable car, running along a different peak.

She looked down at the pen and notepad on her desk, but didn't write anything down.

"You can't save everyone, Drake."

"I know that," he said impatiently.

"Do you?"

"Write that up in your report. I know I can't save everyone, and I'm proud of the work we did yesterday. It was a big success."

Her eyes narrowed to thin slits. "Don't tell me how to do my job."

He stifled a groan.

"Do it properly, then," he said. "No games. Let me go back to my team. Early fall is a busy time of year for us, and with our commander out of town, we're short one man."

She went on as if he hadn't spoken. "What are your first thoughts after the incident?"

"That I'm never getting on a cable car again, if I can help it," he said. She nodded, and this time she wrote something down.

He fielded her questions for a while. Isolde was like a dog with a bone, coming at the problem, or what she thought might be the problem, from several angles at once.

Finally, Drake stood up, running his fingers along his hair.

"I don't understand how you do what you do. Our team rescued thirty people last week, but you won't have heard of those rescues, because everybody survived. It must be hard to only get involved when rescues go south, when we fail to do our job."

He saw by the way she gripped her pen tighter that he'd struck a chord. She inhaled slowly, then came up fighting. "That's not how I see it. Let's go back to yesterday's events. The two men you rescued yesterday are doing fine. I'd just gotten off the phone with their doctor before you arrived."

He sighed theatrically. "You know what I mean. The only reason you're involved is because I happened to be the one out there. I imagine the colonel, or somebody who knows what happened six years ago, called you and asked you to come out."

She didn't bother denying it.

"You keep bringing up that other incident," she said carefully. "Do you want to talk about what happened then, Drake?"

"No."

"Okay," she said easily. "How do you feel today? Any unusual symptoms of stress? Restlessness, insomnia, irritability?"

He cocked an eyebrow at her.

"Greater than normal irritability," she clarified.

"I slept like a baby last night, Doc." He paused briefly. Once again, she didn't call him out on the use of the nickname. Instead, she looked at him in that careful, considerate way of hers—just waiting for him to say something else.

Drake stood his ground. This was a game two could play.

Isolde

"How can I be sure you're not just lying to me? I know how badly you want to get back to your team."

He nodded, staring down at his hands for a moment. When he looked back up at her, his eyes shone like twin pieces of ice on his chiseled face.

"I'm okay." His voice was deep, strong, confident. She stared at his lips for an instant, remembering what it'd felt like to kiss those lips—what it'd felt like to have those strong arms wrapped around her.

Isolde dug her nails into her palms, berating herself for her wholly inappropriate thoughts. It'd been wrong of her to sleep with him six years earlier. She should have stopped seeing him as a patient first.

27

She should have informed the colonel that they were—

But it was too late to do any of that.

Suddenly, she wanted to ask him why he'd never said anything. She knew Drake had felt betrayed when her report had been released—he didn't know it wasn't finished, and that she'd never meant for it to get out like that. At that point, he could have destroyed her career just by telling someone they'd slept together. He could have gotten her fired—maybe even worse. But he'd said nothing to anyone, as far as she could tell.

"What?" he asked gruffly. "You've run out of questions? Does that mean we're done here?"

She bristled at his tone.

"I don't want to fight you, Drake. I'm here to support you."

"Then clear me, so I can get back to work," he said, his voice softer than she'd ever heard it. "Please, Isolde."

Isolde considered Drake carefully for a moment. The fact was, he seemed to be doing ok. More than that, she had the feeling the two of them talking further about what happened wouldn't help him, or not half as much as getting back to his team would.

She took in a big breath. "Okay. I'm going to clear you."

He turned so fast his leg struck her desk.. Her ceramic coffee cup went over the edge. Quick as a flash, his hand reached out, stilling the cup. He placed it carefully back on the desk.

"Sorry," he apologized. His eyes went to the doorway—he looked ready to run out of her office.

"Please let me finish. I said I'm going to clear you, but I need you to do two things for me."

"Anything," Drake said, but his eyes narrowed down suspiciously.

"I need you to promise you'll come see me if you feel any of the symptoms we've discussed."

He nodded quickly. "I promise," he said, his expression earnest. "And the second thing?"

"I want you to come to the hospital with me to meet the men you saved yesterday."

"Is that really necessary?"

"I'd like you to see them. It'll be good for all three of you, I think."

"Is this about closure again?"

"Call it what you will. Should we go over now, or would you prefer to go home, take a day off, and we continue our little chat tomorrow?"

She waited patiently. They both knew she held all the cards in her hand.

"You win, Doc. Lead the way."

She picked up her black leather handbag. "Let's go. My car's in the underground parking."

Neither of them spoke until they were inside her car, on the way to the hospital.

"This is your car?" he asked, with a tone of disbelief. "It should be on its way to the scrapyard, if not there already."

Isolde shrugged lightly, her hands on the faded leather of her Volkswagen Golf's steering wheel.

She wasn't about to tell Drake that this car had been her father's last gift to her. He'd given it to her the day she turned eighteen, along with the promise to teach her to drive it. That promise he hadn't been able to keep—he'd been diagnosed with pancreatic cancer just a few weeks later, and had died gently and quietly, the way he'd always lived.

Leaving a hole the size of Mars in our family.

The car had already been a second-hand vehicle at the time, and that had been fifteen years earlier. Now there was more rust than paint on its body. So yes, perhaps it was time to start thinking about getting a new car. But that wasn't something she wanted to think about.

"I agree it might have seen better days—but never mind my car."

"Is this thing even roadworthy in winter?" he insisted. Beyond his obvious amusement at her choice of vehicle, his voice held traces of real concern.

"I've invested in winter tires for it, if that's what you mean," Isolde said defensively, though she knew exactly what he was asking. She didn't use her car much in winter, for precisely that reason.

He raised his hands, palms up, in surrender. "Okay, Doc. There must be a story here. Maybe someday you'll share it with me."

"Maybe," she said, taking the turn towards the hospital.

For its size, the town of Chamonix had an impressive hospital, with solid equipment, an amazing staff, and a strong specialty in mountaineering and skiing-related trauma injuries.

By the time she parked the car in the visitors' parking area, Drake's shoulders were up by his ears.

"Are you okay?"

He visibly forced himself to relax. "I don't like hospitals much."

"Because of your leg?"

"Because I don't like them," he said gruffly. "Stop trying to psychoanalyze me, Doc."

Isolde stopped to speak with the nurse at the reception, explaining who she was and what she wanted. A couple minutes later, a doctor came out. He was a tall, handsome man in his early forties, with warm brown eyes and a ready smile.

"Dr. Matthieu?" she said, looking up at his nametag.

The doctor nodded, smiling with both his mouth and his eyes. "Yes. And you must be Dr. Durant."

"Isolde, please," she said, nodding. Beside her, Drake made some kind of choking sound, but when she looked at him he was completely still. His hand rubbed his right thigh reflexively—he probably didn't even realize he was doing it.

"Isolde," the doctor agreed. "And you can call me Robert." He turned to include Drake in the conversation. "You must be Lieutenant Jacobs. Both of my patients asked about you as soon as they woke up."

Drake's scowl deepened, but he pushed his hand out to shake the doctor's proffered hand.

"So, you'd like to see Messieurs Martin et Nicolas Blanchard?"

"The two patients are related?" she asked, surprised.

"They are brothers," Dr. Matthieu clarified. "They've authorized me to speak to the police about their injuries, so I can tell you anything you need to know. I've also already sent everything on to the *gendarmerie*, as requested."

"We're just here to see them, if that's okay," Isolde said quickly.

"Of course. Follow me, please."

They walked into a beige room with three beds. The bed closer to the door was empty—the others held two men. The man closest to the window had his leg rigged up on a pulley system—she couldn't help noticing how Drake's expression tightened at the sight of the device.

Shit.

She watched him get control of himself with real effort, shifting his eyes to the other bed, occupied by a man with thick bandages around his head and torso.

Both men looked asleep. Although they were large men, their faces were round and smooth—very similar, in fact, to that of the slightly older man who currently occupied an armchair by the window. He was wearing jeans and a shirt, so he wasn't a patient here.

An older brother?

As soon as he saw them, he slid out of a chair and walked towards them, a strained expression on his round face.

"My brothers need rest," he said, confirming Isolde's assumption.

"*Monsieur* Blanchard, these are Lieutenant Drake Jacobs, from the *Peloton de Gendarmerie de Haute Montagne*, and Dr. Durant, a police psychologist," Dr. Matthieu began.

The man's mouth dropped open in surprise, making his face even rounder. He immediately reached out and clasped Drake's hand, pulling hard enough to bring the larger man towards him.

"*Monsieur* Jacobs, my name is Alain Blanchard. Thank you for coming, thank you. And thank you for saving my brothers." The man's eyes filled with tears, and still he didn't let go of Drake's hand. "I cannot say it enough."

Drake's chiseled face looked cast in stone. He stood still for a moment, then started pulling slowly, trying to extricate his hand from the older man's grip.

She brought her attention back to Alain Blanchard, who was still talking. "My brothers and I were together that morning. I wasn't feeling well, so I never got on the cable car. And to think, if it wasn't for you, I could have lost them both ... it doesn't bear thinking about."

Drake finally freed his hand and patted the other man gently on the shoulder. "I'm glad they are both okay. They will make a full recovery?" he asked.

"They will. Thanks to *you*."

Drake shrugged lightly. "It was just luck that those trees stopped the cabin's fall."

Alain Blanchard's look suddenly went sharp. "I am not altogether a stupid man. You stepped inside that cabin, knowing it could keep sliding any moment, and you got my brother Martin out. Then you went back for Nico and did the same."

A cold sweat broke out on Isolde's forehead. She was being foolish—she'd known perfectly well that Drake had risked his life to get those men out of the wreck. But to picture what would have happened if the cabin had slid while Drake was inside ... it made Isolde's heart ache in a way she wasn't willing to examine right now.

"Are you okay, Isolde?" asked a solicitous Dr. Matthieu. "Do you need anything?"

Clearly observant, the doctor.

"I'm fine, thank you. It's just a bit warm in here," she excused.

Drake's eyes narrowed as he looked at her, but it was Blanchard who strode up to the window and cracked it open, letting in some fresh air.

"I'm glad your brothers are okay," Drake said awkwardly.

Alain Blanchard looked like he was going to jump into Drake's arms, but thought better at the last minute. "Your superiors will get a letter from me, *Monsieur* Jacobs. What you did for my family will not be forgotten."

Drake nodded tightly. He seemed to be begging Isolde with his eyes to get him out of here, so she said their goodbyes, leaving the doctor alone with Alain Blanchard.

"God. Please don't *ever* make me do that again," Drake said when they were back out in the corridor, the door closed behind them.

Isolde laughed. "You saved his family, Drake. He has a right to be grateful."

"All I did was my job, Isolde. I don't need his gratitude—though I'm glad to hear the two will make a full recovery. Moving a rescue is always a hard choice—there's a chance you'll hurt them worse by moving then, but in this case, it was—"

"A necessity," she completed for him.

Drake nodded.

A large figure ran towards them. Before Isolde could wrap her head around what was happening, Drake had placed himself in front of her. She felt the tension in his large frame as he faced the potential threat. A moment later, he relaxed and stood back sheepishly as a uniformed policeman stopped beside them.

"Sorry, Drake, didn't mean to startle you."

"It's okay, Hugo," Drake said. Both men clearly knew each other. "Dr. Isolde Durant, meet *Gendarme* Hugo Morant, from the *Compagnie d'Annecy*. Hugo and I sometimes train in the gym together," Drake added, for her benefit.

Hugo let out a sharp laugh. "Is that what you call it when I kick your ass?"

"Don't get cocky, Hugo, or we'll have to meet again soon," Drake said, his expression relaxed for the first time all day. "What are you doing here?"

"I'm part of the team in charge of investigating the crash. Thanks to you, we actually have some witnesses."

Drake nodded, his expression serious now. "Was it a technical malfunction?"

"If it was, we can't find any trace of it. I was going to come see you this afternoon, but, since you're here already, I'll ask you now. Did you see or hear anything before it happened, Drake?"

Drake shook his head—then stopped. "Maybe a hissing sound. Yes, there was a loud hissing sound—that's why I looked up above the trees, and that's when I saw the cable car fall."

Hugo nodded and wrote something down on his pad. "We'll check it out. I have to go, Drake. Glad to see you in one piece, man."

Isolde and Drake watched the man leave. Finally, Drake turned towards her.

"Now—is it okay if I go over and see my team?"

Isolde nodded. She didn't want Drake to leave, but that had nothing to do with his psychological readiness to get back to his work.

"I can drop you off at the office again," she said.

Drake's lips curled up in a slight smile. She loved how his eyes wrinkled at the corner and all iciness seemed to flow out of them.

"With all due respect, Doc, that tin can's a real danger. I think I'm safer walking."

4

Drake

Drake didn't need to look up from the papers in front of him to know Isolde had just walked into the room. It wasn't anything he could put his finger on—he'd simply always felt her presence keenly, which was one of the reasons it'd been so easy to avoid her for almost six years, even though they'd worked in the same building.

Today she was wearing a dark suit with a silky turquoise top underneath. Her dark hair fell in loose waves around her shoulders, held back from her eyes by an invisible clip. It was a professional look, but it was also sexy as hell.

There were several chairs available at the enormous, oval conference table, and it didn't escape

Drake's notice that she chose the one furthest away from him.

Including Isolde, there were five people sitting at the table. It was what management liked to refer to as a multidisciplinary team: he and Jens Melkopf, from the PGHM, Hugo Morant and another gendarme Drake didn't know from the *Compagnie d'Annecy*, Vincent Morgan, the gendarmerie's public relations' expert, and Yvette Legrand, the mayor's chief of staff. And of course. Isolde.

Although they were still waiting for Colonel Pelegrin to arrive so the meeting could formally begin, the presence of Vincent Morgan and Yvette Legrand already told Drake everything he needed to know about the meeting's objective: to stop the cable crash case from becoming a shitshow for the *gendarmerie* and for the mayor's office.

Drake wished himself anywhere but here. He wanted to be out in the mountains with his team—not stuck in this airless room talking about something that couldn't be undone.

Though he purposefully didn't look at Isolde, he was hyperaware of her presence. He was glad he was sitting down—his cock had gone semi-hard the moment she arrived into the room.

He and Isolde had gone almost six years without speaking more than a couple words to each other—from the moment she betrayed his trust by submitting that file to his superiors, just a few weeks after the first cable car crash, to the moment last weekend when she'd shown up at the second rescue scene.

Normally, Drake wasn't the kind of man to hold a grudge for six years. But he'd been in love with Isolde, so her betrayal had cut him deep.

He'd convinced himself that was all he felt for her—pain at her betrayal. But now that they'd spoken again, now that they were in the same room again, he was shocked to discover just how badly he wanted to get to know her again.

He realized he'd never stopped thinking about Isolde, and silently apologized to every woman he'd dated since then.

He raised his eyes and found her looking at him. Her eyes were warm honey, but her look was wary—like she wasn't quite sure what to think about him.

The door opened again, and the colonel walked in. He stopped them with a wave of his hand as they all attempted to rise.

Colonel Pelegrin was in his mid-forties. Although he was responsible for the entire Chamonix gendarmerie—including two PGHM teams, a team of city gendarmes, and all the support resources and infrastructure—as well as the relationship with the mayor's office, he never looked stressed. He was one of those men who made you feel, when he was talking with you, that you were contributing to something important.

"Ladies, gentlemen, thank you for joining me

today." He did a quick, efficient round of introductions. "We're here to talk about the Brévent incident."

"The mayor is very worried, Colonel. It's been three days already, and we still don't seem to know much," said Yvette Legrand. She was a slim young woman with dark, curly hair and a cream-colored suit that perfectly complemented her dark skin. Drake understood why the mayor needed someone like her by his side—she looked like she could go from this meeting straight to holding a press release without batting an eye.

"Thank you for that context, Ms. Legrand," the colonel said coldly.

Drake knew the man's irritation was directed at the mayor, who hadn't even bothered to join this meeting, and not at his chief of staff.

"Take us through the details, please, *Gendarme* Morant."

Hugo Morant cleared his throat nervously. "We have found no discrepancies in the maintenance logs. The maintenance technician has a stellar record and over thirty years' of experience. I have the full detail here," he said, pointing at his laptop, "but, to summarize, the maintenance log is solid, and shows there had been absolutely no problems with the car before the morning of October 6th."

"So, what you're saying is, it's nothing like the last cable car incident," Yvette Legrand interrupted coldly.

Drake clenched his teeth, feeling the pressure vibrate all the way through his skull.

Incident was certainly one way to refer to it.

Even though his eyes didn't move from the file in front of him, Drake felt the colonel and Isolde staring at him.

It was the colonel who finally replied.

"We have found no safety measure violations in this case," he said carefully. "There is absolutely no reason to believe the two cases might be related."

"And you don't think the press is going to link the two incidents?" Yvette Legrand asked.

Six years ago, a younger maintenance technician had deactivated the emergency braking system, after discovering it kept malfunctioning and interrupting the service. That single, ill-fated decision, had precipitated the crash that killed a little girl.

The pressure in Drake's skull grew. He must have made some kind of sound, for Yvette turned her sharp eyes towards him.

"It seems you're the common link between the two incidents, Lieutenant Jacobs."

Drake had to force his jaw open so he could speak. "I hope you're not implying I had anything to do with the accident, Ms. Legrand," he said coldly.

The woman raised a perfectly manicured hand. "No, no, of course not. I just mean, you were present at both incidents. The press will come find you if they make the connection."

Ah, that's what's bothering you.

He sighed. He could easily reassure her there. "Trust me, I won't be speaking to any reporters."

"You'll send them my way?" she said.

"Actually, Yvette, Lieutenant Jacobs should ask any reporters to speak with *me*," Vincent Morgan said, speaking up for the first time.

Drake relaxed and sat back to watch the pissing contest. His money was on the mayor's chief of staff, but Vincent Morgan could be like a dog with a bone when he set his mind on something, so—

"Lieutenant Jacobs will come to me first if any reporters reach out to him," the colonel said, breaking up the argument. "I'll be the one deciding what to do."

Drake nodded in acknowledgement. That certainly made sense to him. He didn't get paid to deal with this shit.

"In the meantime, let's focus on our current problems. I'd like the two of you to work together on a statement about Sunday's crash," the colonel continued, addressing Yvette and Vincent. Though quiet, his voice left no room for argument. "Dr. Durant, have you spoken to everybody at the scene? Do you have any concerns, or any follow-ups in mind? Anything we should be thinking about?"

Isolde nodded, looking up from her file. "I've spoken to everybody who was at the scene, and don't have any concerns. Everybody knows to come see me if they experience any issues later on."

Drake was inexplicably grateful Isolde didn't use the word *incident* to refer to the first cable car crash.

The meeting went on for an extra fifteen minutes,

but Drake was only half-paying attention. Most action items were focused on preserving the town's brand and reputation, a topic that had nothing to do with him, and one in which he had absolutely no interest.

Finally, the meeting broke up. Drake waited until everybody had left the room before standing up and stretching his creaking leg gratefully.

A second later, Isolde popped her head back into the room.

Drake looked behind him at the empty conference room table to see if she'd forgotten anything.

She shook her head. "I just wanted to speak with you for a minute," she said softly. "Are you okay?"

Her beautiful eyes shone with kindness and intelligence.

Drake clenched his hands to stop himself from pulling back that loose strand of hair falling over her eyes. To cover his need, he huffed impatiently. "I'm fine. You don't need to babysit me."

Her eyes narrowed for an instant. "I'm not babysitting you. I'm just asking you, one colleague to another, if there's anything I can do to help."

"I'm fine. I'd love to stay and chat," he said, making it clear that he'd like that about as much as a trip to the dentist, "but I need to get back to my team now. If you'll excuse me," he said, exiting the room quickly. Her soft, floral scent hit him as he walked past her. It was a familiar, inviting, delicious smell. He had to stop himself from going back.

5

Drake

Sitting in the helicopter with his team, it was difficult to believe that just half an hour earlier he'd been sipping lukewarm coffee in a meeting room. This was his second intervention of the day, but the sixth for his team.

Drake looked at Kat, who'd been working non-stop the entire shift. She looked exhausted. She'd just dropped Jens, Hiro and Bailey off to go pick up some hikers, and was now taking him and Gael to pick up a couple of stranded climbers.

"Hey, Kat," Drake said into his headset. "After this, you need to take a break."

Kat didn't bother looking at him. "I think we all do. Maybe if people give us a break and stop getting dinner?"

"Yeah," Drake agreed, but made a mental note to get Kat home after this one.

He stretched his long legs, trying to relieve some of the tension that was gathering in his muscles—particularly in his right leg. He'd never told anyone that the pain in his leg had never actually disappeared. It'd faded—to the point where, on good days, he could forget about it but, after a hard day like today, his leg liked to remind him of the trauma it'd endured.

On the seat across from him, Gael leaned back with his eyes closed. Drake wondered if his colleague had managed to go to sleep like that. He wouldn't put it past Gael—the man was a world-renowned climber, and had slept in places far worse than this. He'd let him rest for a few more minutes. Then Gael spoke.

"So, tell me about the climbers. We don't have Jens with us, so it can't be too bad?"

"I hope we can take care of it ourselves. Two British climbers were unlucky enough to be caught in a rockfall on the Goûter corridor. One of them is hurt. It was the partner who called us."

"Shit."

Drake nodded in agreement, even though Gael couldn't see him. "Usually rockfalls happen in July and August, during heatwaves, but it's been happening later and later in the last couple of years."

Gael raised his head, opening his bright green

eyes, a contrast against his tanned complexion. "Rémy warned me about this just last week. He and his colleagues have started avoiding the Goûter corridor wherever possible."

Though Drake didn't know Rémy well personally, the mountain guide and avalanche forecaster from St. Gervais had often helped their team, and there were few people in the area who knew more about these mountains than Rémy.

"I'll speak to the colonel about this when we're back."

"Good luck, Drake. I'd be surprised if he didn't already know—there's no chance the mayor's going to want to block off one of Chamonix's main attractions."

"You know how many shits I give about what the mayor wants," Drake grumbled.

"Gentlemen, we're getting close. I'm going to drop you off on the entrance to the couloir—you should be able to hike your way to the climbers from there. I'll wait for you."

Drake nodded. "Dispatch has been in touch with the climbers?"

"They're expecting you," Kat said.

There was no more talk as Kat took the helicopter down gently. Drake looked out the window at the small clearing where she was planning on setting them down.

The woman can land this thing on a coin.

As soon as the helicopter touched down, Drake

and Gael jumped out, shouldering their large packs. The two men didn't speak as they scrambled up to the spot where the climbers had called it in. They pushed themselves hard, knowing every minute could make the difference between life and death.

Finally, Drake saw them. His gaze was caught first by the crimson stream painted onto the rock face. He could see exactly where the climber had fallen.

Fuck. That's a lot of blood.

He dragged his eyes away and sought eye contact with the climbers. One was lying flat on the ground, covered by a thin blue jacket. Beside him, his partner kneeled, whispering to his injured friend. Around them were a bunch of rocks, ranging in size from golf balls to tennis balls.

Drake and Gael kneeled next to them.

"My name is Drake Jacobs, and this is Gael León, from the PGHM. We're here to help. Can you tell me what happened?"

"Thank God you're here. Rocks started falling everywhere... one hit me on the head and I ... I dropped Liam."

"You didn't drop me," the one on the ground mumbled. "You caught me."

Drake and Gael exchanged a glance.

He's not just conscious but aware of what happened. That's good.

"You hit your head against the rocks," his partner sobbed.

There was true fear in the climber's eyes. He

might not have been the one to fall, but in a way watching your partner get hurt, knowing you hadn't been able to stop it from happening, was worse.

This was the darker side of the mountains Drake loved so much—a shadowy side where the mountains could take the life of the very people who loved them most.

Not today, though.

"He was c-cold. I gave him my jacket," the kneeling man said.

"Good. I'm going to take the jacket off now, so we can examine you, Sir," Gael said in a gentle voice.

The man's leg didn't look broken, but it was bleeding heavily. While Gael put pressure on the wound, Drake unpacked the rolled-up tactical stretcher from his backpack.

While they worked, Drake called Kat. "We're at the scene," he said, speaking quietly. "Patient is conscious, with a head and leg injury. The other climber is unhurt, but likely in shock."

"Is it safe to bring him down the trail?" Kat asked, all business.

"Affirmative."

Working together in a well-practiced move, Drake and Gael carefully transferred the patient to the stretcher. They worked quickly and quietly, ignoring the man's pained moans. They couldn't risk giving him anything for the pain before a doctor examined him, so the only chance of making him more comfortable was getting him to the hospital as quickly as possible.

"Are you okay to walk, Sir?" Drake asked, speaking to the other climber. Getting the injured climber out was their top priority, but if needed one of them could huff it back later for the second climber.

The climber nodded and stood on shaky feet. "I'm okay. I'll keep up. But what if we bump into the cat?"

"The cat?" Drake and Gael exchanged a look. It sounded like the man on the stretcher wasn't the only one who needed to get to the hospital.

"The enormous cat that raced by us when the rocks started falling."

Unlikely.

"I'm not making it up," he insisted.

Drake was about to ask the injured climber if he'd seen anything, but the man had fainted.

Probably best. The walk isn't going to be pleasant.

"We'll look into it, Sir," Drake said, feeling proud of his diplomatic answer.

He and Gael lifted the stretcher in tandem, careful to jostle the patient as little as possible.

"We're on our way back, Kat," Drake said. "Be ready for takeoff in ten minutes."

"Roger that."

6

Drake

Drake took a sip of his ice tea. People often asked him why he didn't drink, wondering if there was some sordid history of alcoholism in his family. The truth wasn't half as interesting—Drake liked to be fully in control, and he wasn't about to ingest anything that took that control away from him.

The full team was out tonight—minus Damien, of course. Kat sat down across from him, a small beer in her hand. She still looked tired, but was a bit more relaxed now. Jens had promised he'd drop her off at home when they were done—the doctor also wasn't drinking. Gael and Hiro sat at either end of the table.

"What the hell was that about, this afternoon?" Gael asked, shaking his head.

"The rockfall?" Drake said.

Gael shook his head. "Nah, not that. One of our rescues today claimed he'd seen a large cat by the Goûter couloir."

"That's impossible. Maybe it was a Chamois," Hiro suggested.

"I was worried Drake was going to blow a fuse, but he just told him we'd look into it."

"Very politically correct of you, Drake. Damien will be proud when he gets back."

"The guy was in shock. I'm not sure he knew what he was saying," Drake said, eager to change the subject.

Normally, Drake enjoyed unwinding with his friends after work. They didn't get together that often, but once a week or so somebody would suggest a drink, and Drake was usually one of the first to show up.

Today, however, his heart wasn't in it. Instead of celebrating the six successful interventions earlier that day, he couldn't stop thinking about the fucking cable car. And not the one from a couple days earlier—that, at least, would have made some amount of sense. But his mind kept going back to the accident six years earlier.

And to the little girl with brown curly hair, who'd died.

He wasn't an idiot. Seeing that cable car fall on Sunday had opened the Pandora's box of his mind. There was no going back now—it was on his mind day and night.

"Are you sure you're okay, Drake?" Kat asked.

Gael cocked his head. "Drake's just being his usual, broody self."

"I don't know, I think he's somehow broodier than usual."

"Stop talking about me like I'm not here, guys," Drake said, but he softened his tone. These were his friends, his team. "I'm okay. I think I just need a bit of fresh air."

He stood up, careful not to jostle the table, and walked outside. It was definitely easier to breathe out here.

Drake was trying to decide whether he should go back inside or call it a night and go home. He lived right in the center of town, so he could walk there in a matter of minutes. He kicked a small rock on the ground—soon, everything would be covered in snow.

Suddenly, a flash went off to his left—he flinched before realizing it was a tourist taking a picture across the street, and not the press. Ever since Yvette Legrand had mentioned it, he'd been expecting the press to come after him. Eventually, they would link this cable car crash to the one that happened six years earlier.

"You okay, Drake?" Hiro asked. Drake hadn't even noticed his friends had followed him out. Beside Hiro stood Bailey—the black Dutch Shepherd was Hiro's constant companion. In Chamonix, dogs were allowed almost everywhere, which was good because

Hiro probably wouldn't set foot in any establishment where Bailey wasn't allowed as well.

The words were out before Drake could stop them. "I thought it was a reporter."

"Why would a reporter be interested in you, Drake?" Gael asked.

Behind him, Jens and Hiro made a strangled noise. Drake would have laughed, if the whole thing hadn't been so damn sad. Everybody was always so careful not to mention the incident to him.

He didn't bother replying. He wondered what it was like for the girl's family now. The parents had started their holiday as a family of four and had gone home a few days later with one child and a broken heart.

The girl's older brother had been closer to the cabin window. Drake had pulled him out first—he'd handed the boy over to Damien, then gone back in for the little girl.

She'd been conscious but terrified, huddled against the back corner of the cabin, lying on what used to be the roof. He'd only just dragged himself inside when the structure had collapsed on top of them—crushing his leg and her thorax at the same time.

He'd read the autopsy report. He knew the girl had died as a result of blunt thoracic trauma—what the report didn't say was that she died because Drake hadn't been fast enough or strong enough to get her out.

If he'd only been one second faster, if he'd been able to wedge his hips into the small space, he might have been able to protect her long enough for Damien and the rest of the team to get her out.

Or you both would have died.

That's what Isolde had told him, over the course of the multiple conversations they'd had together on the topic—conversations which had, in due course, led to other, more pleasurable things.

Before she betrayed you.

"I feel like I'm missing something," Gael said, doggedly.

"You guys can tell him and Kat about it," Drake said. "It's not a big secret. You should all know, anyway, in case the press do come looking after me."

"What are you going to do?" Jens asked. The doctor's warm brown eyes were fully of worry.

"I'm going to head home and get some sleep."

"I don't know what's going on, Drake, but call us if you need anything," Gael asked. *"Para eso están los amigos."*

Drake nodded, but he had no intention of bothering his friends with this. Precisely because they were friends, and because this wasn't their cross to bear.

It's mine.

7

Isolde

A young man in the third row looked at his watch—never an encouraging sign for a speaker. Isolde took a deep breath and looked around the room quickly, relieved to find most people were still nodding and making eye contact.

Time to wrap this up.

She usually enjoyed her Thursday lunch-time sessions with new trainees. They joined the *gendarmerie* with fresh ideas and high hopes and, while it wasn't her job to scare them, it *was* her job to make sure they knew where they could turn to for help, should they need it.

Today, however, she was having trouble concentrating. Her thoughts kept going back to Drake. Four days had gone by since the crash, and the topic was finally dying in the news. It looked like the mayor and his chief of staff had been hard at work making sure the town's reputation wasn't affected. But that wasn't Isolde's concern. She was worried about Drake, and how bleak he'd looked the last time she'd seen him, at the meeting with the mayor the day before.

She hoped she'd done the right thing by clearing him so quickly. It had felt like the right thing to do, but—

One of the trainees put up her hand to ask a question.

"Will our boss find out if we go speak with you?" a young woman asked from the first row.

Isolde shook her head quickly, glad for the question, and answered it honestly, to the best of her ability.

The perception that anything they shared might not be confidential was the number one barrier preventing police officers from seeking counseling. And, of course, Isolde had done a lot of thinking on this topic after the debacle with Drake's file six years earlier.

She's often thought of what she could have done differently in that case—excepting the obvious, of course, as she and Drake should never should have slept together in the first place, or at least not before telling their superiors about it. That had been a breach of ... everything.

Isolde *had* taken steps to ensure Drake was

informed of the laws pertaining to confidentiality and privilege, and made sure he understood what the information he shared with her during their sessions together would be used for. What she hadn't been able to do, due to a combination of IT and human error, was to warn him, before the dossier went out, that she would be recommending further time off for him.

He'd taken the formal recommendation as a punishment, and, furthermore, a personal betrayal. She'd tried to apologize, but Drake had ignored all her calls and, she assumed, deleted all her messages. He'd never given her the chance to explain.

Over time, she'd convinced herself she was over him—except she knew she was lying to herself. It was obviously too late now to pick up that relationship where they'd left it off, but her body didn't care about that. It wanted to be closer to him.

There were no further questions, so Isolde wrapped up the session and headed outside. In the corridor, she almost tripped over a dark shadow.

"Bailey!" she said, reaching out to rub the dog's dark head. She looked up to see Hiro Habu, Bailey's dog handler and a member of the PGHM, striding quickly in their direction. She looked behind him to make sure Drake wasn't there as well, as she didn't think she could bear to bump into him again. But the corridor was empty.

"Sorry, Dr. Durant. She knows it's time to head home," Hiro apologized.

There's a man who won the genetic lottery.

He was tall and lean, with golden skin and dark, soulful eyes. She'd heard someone mention his mother was Japanese and his father French—they must have both been very good-looking. But his good looks didn't faze her—only one man in this building managed that.

Isolde laughed. "Good for you, Bailey. I'm going home as well as soon as I wrap up a couple files."

Bailey made a strange, purring noise that made her sound more like a cat than a dog.

"You like that, huh," Isolde said, rubbing the soft fur under her neck gently.

"Careful, Doctor, or you'll be here all night," Hiro said, smiling more with his eyes than his mouth.

A few minutes later, opening the door to her office, Isolde realized she was smiling. Bailey was, by far, the best destresser.

8

Isolde

He jinxed me.
Drake jinxed me by talking about my car like that.

Isolde hit the steering wheel with her open palm, then turned the key in the ignition one more time. No luck. Her dear, stupid car simply wouldn't start.

Tears filled her eyes—she tried blinking them away. She knew herself well enough to know it wasn't the thought of walking home that was upsetting her so—she could walk home in under fifteen minutes and have a mechanic come tomorrow to the parking garage to look at her car. Luckily tomorrow was a Friday, rather than the weekend.

But the thought of having to say goodbye to that

car, that was something she wasn't ready for—something she didn't think she'd ever be ready for.

Breathe in. Breathe out. There you go.

Slowly, she started feeling more in control. She leaned her forehead gently onto the steering wheel and kept talking to herself.

It's going to be okay. Everything's going to work out.

Instants later, a voice shattered that control.

"Isolde?"

No. Go away.

The temptation to ignore the voice was strong, but Isolde knew Drake wasn't simply going to walk away. His voice was laced with concern.

She opened the car door. His large, veined hand grabbed on to it and pulled it all the way open. His strong hands, with their neatly clipped nails, were one of the first things she'd noticed about him.

"Is everything okay, Isolde?"

Years of working together in the same building and successfully avoiding each other, and now she couldn't seem to go two steps without bumping into him. It was wreaking havoc on her concentration.

He was still waiting for her to answer the question.

"My car won't start."

Drake's full lips turned into a slight smile.

"Don't say it," she begged. "Please don't say it." Once again, the tears threatened to fall.

He raised his hands, palms up, towards her. "Hey … hey … it's okay. I can drive you home. Leave the car here tonight, we'll get someone in to look at it tomorrow morning."

It's what she'd been planning on doing, anyway.

"Thanks, it's okay, I can walk. I don't live too far away."

"Let me drive you. It'll give you the chance to pick at my brain a bit more, if you like."

She couldn't help but smile at that.

"I'm off duty. I wasn't planning on picking at any brains tonight. Just pizza and Netflix."

"Is that an invitation?"

What?

She assumed her mouth was hanging open, so closed it quickly.

"No, but I'll accept the lift."

Drake's car was a large Toyota SUV. The tough, powerful vehicle suited him—she didn't imagine it had any trouble navigating Chamonix's winter weather.

As they drove past her much smaller car, Isolde shot a dejected look.

"Don't worry, we'll send someone to look at it tomorrow morning," Drake said.

"I submitted the report today." Isolde saw Drake's hands tense on the steering wheel. After a second, they visibly relaxed.

"So, I'm not your patient anymore," he said quietly.

"No. Though I still think you should see a psychologist if—"

"Could I see *you*?"

She shook her head hard. "No. Not me. My colleague, when he gets back from holiday. Or I can recommend—"

Drake chuckled. The sound went straight to her stomach, causing it to tighten.

Or maybe somewhere lower.

"Relax, Isolde. I was just kidding." He shot her a quick look, then his eyes went back to the road.

"Why are you looking at me like that?"

"Like what?" he asked.

"I don't know. Like you ..."

"Like I can't get you out of my mind? Maybe because that's exactly what's happening. Even though I should know better."

A part of her, the part she knew she should be listening to, understood Drake had just insulted her—the rest of her unfortunately didn't care.

He still wants me.

He wants me.

She wanted him too. More than she'd ever wanted any man before. It made her realize she'd never stopped wanting him—she'd just convinced herself she had.

"I know you hate me," she began, carefully.

Drake's hands tightened on the steering wheel. Isolde sat back in the comfortable car seat and waited. She wasn't worried that he'd hurt her—that wasn't the kind of man he was.

66

"I don't hate you, Isolde. I was angry, I was hurt. But it was my fault I got my heart broken. Not yours."

Isolde's eyes looked at him in alarm.

His heart?

She'd figured the relationship had meant *less* to him, hence why he'd been able to break it off so easily.

"Let me take you out to dinner, Isolde."

"You want to go out to dinner? Together?"

He nodded, his eyes still on the road. "Clear the air between us. Just as friends."

Drake

Friends my ass.

He didn't want to be Isolde's friend. Or rather, he did, but he wanted to be her friend and wrap himself around those curves of hers at the same time. He wanted to make her come, and learn if she still screamed out her pleasure in bed.

Because as angry as he'd been with her, and as much as he'd tried to stop himself from doing so, he'd never stopped thinking about her. And, despite everything that had happened between them—or maybe *because* of everything that had happened between them, he wanted nothing more than to get to know her again now.

She paused for a moment before shaking her

head no. Drake had expected her to say no, so that small hesitation thrilled him. She wasn't entirely unaffected.

He drove slowly, delaying the inevitable moment when they'd arrive at her place, but Chamonix was a small town. Less than ten minutes after leaving the office, he parked outside her apartment building.

"I'm not going to ask how you know where I live," she said.

"I'm not stalking you, I promise," he said. The thought that she might be scared of him burned a hole into his heart. Isolde seemed to understand. She reached over and placed her smaller palm over his hand as it clenched over the steering wheel. "I would never hurt you."

"I wasn't worried. I know you would never hurt anyone who wasn't a danger to others."

He nodded, relaxing. That seemed like a very fair way of phrasing it.

Isolde picked up her handbag and opened the car door. He didn't want her to step out of the car, but couldn't think of anything to say to keep her there longer. He waited as she got out and turned back towards him.

"Thanks for the lift, Drake," she said tightly.

This is where she says goodnight and you drive away.

"I'll see you around, Isolde," he said, but still couldn't get his finger to press the ignition button.

Isolde's teeth worried her bottom lip—his cock

jumped at the sight. He wanted to be the one between those beautiful lips.

She's going to ask why you're still here.

"Do you want to come upstairs?"

Drake's mouth dropped open in surprise. For a second, he thought he might have misunderstood her.

"Do you want to come up?" she repeated, and while he was glad she'd said it again, so he could stop wondering if he was going crazy, he didn't like the way her voice sounded more hesitant this time.

"Uh ..."

"I'm not looking for a relationship," she said. "But if you want to come upstairs, I'd like that."

He was out of the car before he could question either his sanity or hers.

"You did hear what I said, right? All of it? Also the part where I said I'm not in the market for a boyfriend."

Drake nodded. He'd take any and all her conditions, just to spend five more minutes in her presence.

They rode the elevator in silence to her third-floor apartment. She unlocked the door and pushed it open, walking left towards her kitchen, where she took off her shoes. He followed her example and went back out into the living room in his socked feet.

He decided then and there that he wasn't going to take Isolde to his place. Not that there was anything wrong with his apartment, but it was clearly little more than a place to sleep and shower. Hers was—a home.

From the floating shelves in the living room to the luxurious sofa, everything in her apartment was soft, light and airy. Drake knew immediately that she hadn't hired an interior decorator to achieve this look—no, this was all *her*, and that's what made it a real home.

"I know you don't drink alcohol, but I'm afraid all I have is tap water or skim milk," she said in a halting voice.

He shook his head, bemused.

Maybe she's more nervous than she looks.

"Water's fine."

He heard the cabinets open and close, then the tap turn on. While he waited, he walked over to the balcony where she'd set up her home office. He could easily imagine her working here.

When she joined him in the living room, Drake took the glass she offered but grabbed on to Isolde's wrist with his other hand. He kept his touch loose and gentle, so she could easily move away if she wanted to.

She didn't. She took one step forward until they were standing inches away from each other. Since she'd taken off her heels, she was now a full head shorter than him. Isolde went on tiptoes, raising her face towards him, and still he waited—until she reached up to touch the back of his neck, pulling him down towards her.

She made a little humming sound, and fuck if he didn't remember that exact noise. It went straight to his cock, turning the semi hard-on he'd had since seeing her in the garage into a raging hard-on.

The moment their lips met, Drake understood why he'd been waiting for her for six years—knew also that he would wait forever for her.

He closed his eyes, purposefully keeping the kiss slow and gentle, but that was clearly not what Isolde wanted. Her hand tightened on the back of his neck as her mouth opened further, the tip of her tongue coming out to connect with his. They explored each other's mouth, their bodies so close to each other that Drake couldn't tell if the pounding he was hearing was the sound of his heart or hers.

He could have kissed her for hours, but after only a few minutes she took a step back. Drake didn't have the chance to ask her why before she took his hand and led him out of the living room, into her bedroom.

Like the rest of the apartment, her bedroom was light. A Queen-sized bed was the focus of attention—Drake counted eight pillows in different shades of blue an instant before Isolde closed the bamboo blinds almost all the way, leaving the room in semi-darkness.

"Hey," he complained, reaching for her shape. The complaint died on his lips as his eyes got used to the darkness and he saw her start undoing her button-down blouse.

"That's a lot of buttons," he said breathlessly. "Let me help you."

"Please," she whispered, arching into his touch.

Drake's large hands cupped the weight of her breasts easily—a real handful. His thumbs grazed over her nipples for an instant, before he turned his attention to the buttons. He was as careful with those buttons as he planned on being with her, even though his cock throbbed for attention behind his zipper.

Finally, he pushed the blouse off her shoulders, baring a lacy white balcony bra that had trouble containing her beautiful breasts.

Unable to help himself, he pushed the fabric down and bared a nipple, watching it pebble under his gaze. Staring straight into her eyes, Drake rolled the nipple between thumb and forefinger, until it stiffened to the size of a large, ripe raisin. Then he sucked hard on it.

Her hips jerked towards his.

"Please," she begged.

He raised his mouth from her breast for an instant, just to form the words. "Please, what?" he asked, then went right back to sucking gently.

"More," she said. Her hands went to his shirt. She found the bottom edge of his polo shirt and pulled, scratching him lightly as she did so. Drake helped her get it off, thrilled by the moan of appreciation when his upper body was bared. He wanted more light, so he could see her better—but her touch distracted him, her hands reaching for his belt buckle. Moments later, his pants and boxer shorts were down by his ankles. His cock sprung free, straight and long, seeking only one thing—to be inside her.

He stepped out of his trousers and boxer shorts and took off his socks.

Her small hands ran along his body, caressing his shoulders, his pecs, his stomach muscles. His cock clenched, wondering when its turn was going to come.

"Your body is ... wow," Isolde whispered.

"You're wearing too many clothes," Drake replied. "Come here." He took off her pants. Her panties were made of the same scrappy lace as her bra—fine enough that he could rip it in one easy move. Isolde's breasts heaved, as if she could read his thoughts. She hadn't moved the cups of the bra back, so the cups still hung below her breasts, pushing them out towards him. It was sexy as hell. He wanted to suck on those nipples and never stop.

"You should wear your bra like this all the time," he said, kneading her breasts.

"Take my panties off," she begged.

Keeping one hand on her breasts, Drake moved his other hand down the side of her body. As he touched her stomach, she moved away.

Ticklish?

He ran his fingers down to her hips until their path was stopped by a bit of lace. He pulled it downwards, baring her sex for him. He wished again there were more light in the room. Now that the barrier between them was gone, his fingers found her mound—her hair down there was neat and trimmed, but womanly. Drake moaned appreciatively—he wasn't a fan of the pre-pubescent bare look.

He remembered how they'd touched each other in the past, but six years was a long time. He was going to learn her pleasure tonight, and not make any assumptions about her desire.

Isolde walked towards the bed and he followed—he would have followed her to the ends of the world. He wanted to make this good for her—so good that she came back for more, because he already knew he would want more.

Lying beside her to avoid crushing her, he parted her folds gently. He almost wept for joy as his finger found her wet already for him—he spread her wetness from her slit up to her sensitive clit. She moaned as he slid his thumb across the small nub, again and again.

"Stop, please."

Drake immediately froze and moved up the bed so he could stare into her eyes. *Stop* was a red word for him. "Are you okay, Isolde?"

He needed her to know he would stop at any point if she wanted him to.

"Yes! I didn't mean stop. I meant slow down. If you keep doing that you're going to make me come."

"If I keep doing *this*, you mean?" His thumb went back to its earlier task.

"Yes! Yes! Don't make me come yet, I want us to come together."

"How about you come *now*, and then we come together?" he asked. It wasn't really a question. He kept up the rhythmical gentle strumming on her clit, but added a finger inside her. She was so fucking tight, he was going to have to do a thorough job to prepare her for his cock.

She tensed and her fingers clenched around his arm, sinking into muscle. "Please. Please don't stop," she moaned.

"I have no plans of stopping, Isolde," Drake said. He kept his gentle assault, delighting in the way her breasts rose and fell, her expression pulled tight with arousal.

"More," she begged. He complied, bringing her over the edge. She screamed his name. The walls of her pussy pulsing around his finger, making him wish it were his cock inside her.

Her eyes, when she looked up at him, were glazed with desire. It was sweeter than sex, in a way, because he got to watch her reach her completion, but looking at her now, glazed and sated, he wanted nothing more than to sink himself inside her.

Fuck.

He didn't have a condom on him.

"I have condoms," she said, once again reading his mind. A small smile played on her lips. "Night table."

"Thank God," he whispered, moving over to find one and sheathing himself in record time. When he moved back towards the bed. Isolde was lying with her legs spread open, her knees almost touching the sheets.

His cock jerked at the sight.

"Keep your legs just like that," he grunted.

"I don't think you'll fit otherwise," she said teasingly, but there was a bit of worry in her eyes as well.

"Trust me. I'll fit, and I'll make it good, sweetheart, I promise."

Even if it kills me.

He aligned himself with her entrance and began pushing inside her slowly. In the back of his mind, he knew they'd done this before, but this time felt different.

Was she this tight back then? This hot?

He was only halfway in when he felt her shudder. He immediately stopped.

"Are you okay, Isolde?" The thought of hurting her was like a bucket of cold water.

"Keep going, Drake. You're just ... so much."

His name on her mouth almost made him lose control. He continued, slowly, until he was fully sheathed inside her warmth.

He bent his head down so their foreheads touched and prayed for control. He'd never felt this close to another human being before.

"Oh God, Drake," she whispered.

"Tell me what you need, Isolde," he begged.

"I need ... more."

More I can do.

Drake moved against her. His hips pressed on her pubic bone and she let out a cry that had him seconds again from coming.

"I'm going to come if you do that," she breathed out.

He did it again, and again, holding his own orgasm off through sheer force of will until she finally climaxed.

"Drake!"

Her walls contracted against his cock once, twice, and then he went over the cliff as well, coming harder than he ever had in his life.

"God, Isolde, that was ..."

He wasn't sure what he was going to say, but she stopped his words with a gentle kiss. "It *was*."

Drake wanted to stay inside her forever, but forced himself off her and made his way to the bathroom to take care of the condom. When he came back, she'd crawled under the duvet, leaving one side open for him. He got into bed beside her, undone by the sweet gesture, gathering her close. She was asleep moments later, and it didn't take him long to follow her.

Isolde

"Drake?" Isolde kept her voice purposefully low. "Wake up, Drake, you're having a nightmare."

She'd woken up to find him curled up onto his side, his expression agonized. He was drenched in sweat, his body shaking as his huge arms clenched around his right leg. Her heart broke as she heard him cry out.

She didn't tell him it wasn't real, or any other such platitude. It was real to him, and that was the only thing that mattered. She also didn't touch him, even though every instinct she possessed ached to hold him and make the pain go away.

"Drake," Isolde tried again. "Please wake up."

She reached over and turned on her small bedside lamp, bathing the room in the softest light. She knew the moment he came back to consciousness because his back muscles tensed even further.

"Fuck," he breathed out shakily. He still grabbed on to his ruined calf. A second later, he turned towards her. His nostrils flared as he tried to breathe through the pain, but his voice was steady. "Just a cramp. I'm sorry, Isolde—didn't mean to wake you."

She placed her hand on top of his, then, when he didn't move away, slipped her smaller hand under his larger one, massaging his leg. With her other hand, she pushed his larger body onto his back. He brought his forearm over his eyes.

Ever so slowly, she felt him relax into her touch.

"Thank you," he finally said. "I'm okay now."

She kept her touch purposefully light, maintaining the connection. "Does this happen often?" she asked.

He shrugged, not looking at her. "Once in a while."

She nodded, looking at his leg—the ruined flesh a reminder of the pain he'd gone through.

"You're staring at my leg again. Does the scar bother you that much?"

Isolde sent him a smoldering glance. She knew exactly what he was doing. "You're not going to get rid of me that easily, Drake. You know I don't care about the scar. I just ... I hate seeing how much pain you went through."

"The leg was the least of it. I would have given up the leg in a second if it meant saving that little girl's life."

His words weren't a surprise to her.

"I know that," she said quietly.

It'd been her first time attending a scene. She'd been called out because there were kids involved, and had arrived on the scene moments before the final collapse of the cabin. The image of Drake and the girl trapped under the wreck was branded in fire in her mind, as she knew it must be in the minds of all first responders.

Even with no leverage, his leg pinned down and shattered, Drake had still struggled to lift the metal off the little girl. Isolde's heart broke a little when she thought of what he'd gone through.

"Her parents came to see me at the hospital, you know?" His voice was laced in pain. Isolde pressed herself against his chest.

"You can't take anything they said at face value, they were hurting—"

Drake shook his head. A muscle clenched behind his jaw. "You don't understand. They were *kind* to me—the man who'd let their daughter die. They just wanted to know if ... if she'd died quickly."

"Oh."

"I told them it was quick and painless." His eyes narrowed as a memory hit him. "But it wasn't. She died slowly and in pain, looking right into my eyes."

Drake sat up in bed. His broad shoulders seemed to carry the weight of the world. "I wasn't strong enough to get her out."

"Nobody could have lifted that weight, Drake. You're not Superman." She wished there was something she could say to help him get rid of the guilt, but it was something he was going to have to figure out for himself.

"I don't want to keep talking about it, Isolde."

He's not ready yet.

Isolde nodded. It was probably time to come clean on something else.

"There is something I need to tell you, Drake, about what happened afterwards ... something I've wanted to tell you for a long time." She took a deep breath and squeezed her eyes together—she would not cry. "The file wasn't ready to be sent. It was incomplete. I was going to tell you before submitting—"

Drake interrupted her. "It's okay. You don't need to explain anything, Isolde. It's forgotten."

Forgetting had never been one of her strongest points. Isolde had a great memory—one of the handicaps of having spent so many years at school.

Could it really be that easy?

My biggest regret of the last years, erased, just like that?

"Okay," she said doubtfully. "There's something else I've wanted to ask you for a long time. When the file came out ... why didn't you tell anyone we slept together?"

He shrugged. "How would that have helped?"

Isolde almost laughed. It was impossible to argue against his logic.

"Come here," he said, reaching out for her. He tried to kiss her, but she moved her face to the side.

"Hey, what's wrong?"

"We shouldn't be doing this. We work together."

I promised myself I'd never do this again.

But it feels so right.

He nodded. "Do you want to stop?"

"No. I've missed... this." She'd been about to say *you*, but caught herself at the last minute.

His lips found hers. "I've missed this too. You are so beautiful."

She wasn't—not really. She was too soft, too average. But Drake made her feel what no man had ever made her feel before or since. He made her feel beautiful. He made her feel ... more.

"We shouldn't work together again. I'm going to file a report."

He nodded. "They might ask you why."

"Personal incompatibilities."

"This *is* quite personal," he agreed. "But I think the compatibility is quite high." One corner of his mouth lifted in a crooked smile, and she felt impossibly proud of herself for having put it there.

His hands gently caressed her collarbone, moving down to her breasts and her belly.

She closed her eyes, amazed that somebody so gruff and stoic could also be so tender in bed.

9

Drake

By the time he woke up, Isolde was dressed already—that had been the first sign that she wasn't feeling cuddly. The second had been when she'd kicked him out, without even offering him a cup of coffee.

Drake tried not to take it personally. She hadn't made nor broken any promises. But after their middle-of-the night chat, it's true he'd hoped—

"Hey, Drake! Are you with us?"

Drake nodded sheepishly at Kat. "Sorry, Kat. I'm ready."

He threw his backpack into the helicopter and jumped up, sitting down beside Gael and Jens, who were already waiting. Instants later, they were off.

Drake rotated his shoulders, looking to relax. It'd been a long day, and it was only four p.m. He'd taken part in three extractions, and could have helped out in three more if he hadn't been asked to join two more debrief meetings with the colonel back in the office.

After two weeks of standing in for his friend Damien, the team's commander, Drake couldn't wait for him to get back from his honeymoon. If the last two weeks had taught Drake anything, it's that he didn't want Damien's job. Drake needed action—he needed to be in the thick of things, not talking about them.

A flash of lighting struck outside the helicopter. It'd been raining all day, but the weather was getting worse. He wondered if they were going to make it to the Grand Capucin at all.

"How are things looking, Kat?" he asked.

"Not great, Drake. Visibility is limited. I just heard from the Annecy team pilot, they've had to turn back from the Aiguille du Midi. It's not that bad for us here yet, though."

"Keep me updated, Kat." Drake turned to Jens. "What do you think?"

Jens paused before answering. "I spoke to the hiker who saw the climber fall and called it in. We know where he's lying, and we know he hasn't moved since he fell." Jens's eyes were dark with worry. "I should go,"

"Let me go first," Gael offered. "I'll secure myself

to the wall and help you when you come down with the equipment."

Drake nodded. The helicopter hiccupped in the air, and he had to grab on with both hands to avoid falling. "Are you sure you're both up for this?"

Both men smiled. "You're not losing your nerve on us, are you, Drake? This is what we do."

Drake looked at the men, and at Kat up front. He nodded. They couldn't leave the climber stranded. If there was any chance he was alive, they had to get him out of there before the storm got worse.

The Grand Capucin appeared on their left. Through the rain, the large monolith of vertical granite looked almost black.

"Time to get out there, guys. This is going to get worse before it gets better," Kat said. "I'll keep her steady while you go down, Gael."

Drake clipped himself to the bar on top of the helicopter door. The Allouette wasn't their usual helicopter, but the newer EC 145 had been undergoing a routine maintenance check. This one was smaller, an older model with a less powerful engine. Drake knew Kat could fly any and all available aircraft, so he wasn't worried about that. What did worry him was the fact that the Allouette's winch cable was thirty meters shorter than the usual—which meant Kat would have to fly that much closer to the granite wall as she dropped Gael off.

Gael tightened his rain gear around his head and

hips, then shouldered his pack. Jens rechecked Gael's harness, a standard precaution.

Jens gave Gael a thumbs up sign, which Gael quickly returned. The climber was smiling. "Let's do this."

"You ready, Kat?"

"Ready. I'll keep her steady, just don't stop and enjoy the view, Gael."

Moments later, Gael disappeared from view. Drake kept an eye on the man as he dropped, holding his breath until he dropped onto the ledge. Gael immediately released himself from the cable.

"I'm clipped in," Gael said, speaking into the radio.

"Can you see him?" Jens asked, his voice clipped.

"I see him. He's on his side, not moving."

"The storm's getting worse. I'm going to circle loosely while Gael examines him."

Jens muttered something under his breath. The tall, broad-shouldered man seemed uncharacteristically sullen. "I should have just gone down myself."

"Give Gael a second. He'll—"

"Victim is unconscious and in respiratory distress. Shit, I need Jens here now."

"I'm going down," Jens said, bending down to grab his medical pack. Suddenly, the helicopter lurched, throwing Jens against Drake, who steadied the doctor.

Kat's voice was clipped. "Sorry, guys. This isn't good. Visibility just changed, I don't have a visual reference."

Drake didn't need her to draw a picture for him. Flying a helicopter close to a granite wall was a hazardous enterprise at the best of times, something only a few pilots attempted—but doing it in a storm, without a visual reference, wasn't brave. It was madness.

"I need to get down there now, Drake," Jens insisted.

"Give her a second, Jens. If it's possible, Kat will make it happen."

The rain continued to pummel the helicopter. Kat took them away from the rock and circled at a safe distance.

"What's going on, Jens?" Gael asked. He sounded panicked, and Gael never panicked. "If you don't get here right now, we're going to lose him."

Jens slammed his fist against the side of the helicopter. "Fuck. I should have gone down when we had the chance."

"Guys, I think there's a clearing in the clouds up there. I can try to get close again but it's going to be—"

"Do it," Jens said immediately.

Kat was quiet for a moment.

"Drake?"

She didn't need to say anything else. Drake knew it was his call. He could order her to head back home, and she would. Gael could hunker down until the storm had passed. But a human being would die.

"Drake ... let me go down," Jens begged. The man's jaw was clenched tight.

Drake made his decision. "Do it, Kat."

In a matter of seconds, Jens was clipped into the cable. The doctor swung out of the cabin, into the storm. Drake let the cable out fast. The quicker they got Jens down there and clipped to the rock, the safer he'd be.

"*Merde!*"

Drake heard Kat's loud curse an instant before the helicopter swung sideways, slamming Drake headfirst onto the seat next to him. There was a loud, clattering noise. He tightened his hold on the cable reflexively and straightened back up again.

Drake knew immediately what had happened. As the wind had changed, they'd gotten too close to the wall and the rotor blades had clipped the rock. It was a miracle that they were still in the air.

Kat cursed again as she fought to control the machine.

"We're going to crash, Drake!"

Drake couldn't help her—Kat would have to figure it out on her own. All he cared about was Jens, who was swinging out in space, getting closer and closer to the granite wall. Drake's muscles bunched as he worked double-time to reel Jens back.

Jens is dead if you can't get him back here.

Drake thought of every barbell he'd ever lifted, every push-up and pull-up he'd ever done.

The ground rose to meet them at vertiginous speed.

"I can't keep us in the air! Brace!"

Ignoring Kat's command, Drake pulled and pulled. He couldn't spare the second it would take to look out the window, so he had no idea how far from the helicopter Jens was still.

Suddenly, Jens's body appeared at floor level. Drake let go of the winch and grabbed on to the man's harness, pulling with all his might to bring Jens into the cabin. Knowing they were running out of time, he hugged Jens tight against his own body, tucking the man's head against his chest.

An instant later, the crippled machine struck the ground with a thud.

Drake felt his teeth jar and tasted blood.

Almost bit my tongue off.

He swallowed, disgusted by the metallic taste.

Beside him, Jens groaned.

"Jens?" Drake shook the man in his arms.

"Jesus, Drake. Let me go. I can't breathe."

Drake let out a relieved breath.

Fuck. That was too close.

He realized they hadn't heard any sound coming from the cockpit.

"Kat? Are you okay?"

The pilot walked back towards them. He red hair was loose, rather than in her customary ponytail, and blood dripped down her forehead from where she must have hit her head against the controls on landing, but otherwise she looked unharmed.

"Is this thing going to explode?" Jens asked.

Kat shook her head. "Don't think so. We're okay. How are you both doing?"

"Outstanding landing, Kat," Drake said.

"Yeah, tell that to the colonel," Kat said, laughing.

"Couldn't care less what the colonel thinks," Jens replied. "We shouldn't even be alive."

Outside, the rain continued pummeling the machine.

Now that Drake looked at him carefully, the man seemed a bit uncertain on his feet. There was a goose egg growing on his forehead.

"You hit your head against something," he stated, worried. Head injuries were nothing to laugh about.

"I think I hit the landing skids as you were pulling me up. It's nothing. Thanks, man. You saved my life."

I'm also the reason you almost died.

Drake was saved from having to respond by Gael's frantic voice on their communication device.

"Guys? Tell me you're okay, please."

It was Kat who replied.

"I had to land the helicopter, Gael. We're okay. I'm reaching out to the Annecy team to come pick you up."

She paused for a second. They all knew what she wasn't saying.

A patient in respiratory distress didn't have that kind of time.

90

"I'm sorry, Gael."

Two hours later, Drake leaned back against a different helicopter wall, listening to Beau Fontaine, commander of the Annecy unit, drone on and on about those older helicopters in that gruff voice of his.

"It wasn't the helicopter's fault, Beau. I clipped the rock," Kat insisted.

It must be strange for her to be sitting down back here with them. She'd wanted to stay back with her machine, but the colonel had called them all back. The mechanic wasn't going to be available until the following morning, and nobody wanted Kat to sleep out there.

"While flying the machine in a storm, working to get a man onto that ledge with only a thirty meter winch cable," Drake clarified. "I'm with Beau on this one."

"Come here, Kat," Gael said, reaching out and giving Kat an easy hug. Gael looked exhausted, but his dark green eyes were smiling. Beside them, on a stretcher, the injured climber dozed, supervised by Jens.

Back up in the mountains, when he'd realized the team wasn't going to be able to get them out, Gael had managed the unthinkable. Using only a scalpel, an elastic bougie and an endotracheal tube, he'd performed a surgical cricothyroidotomy and successfully established an airway.

In the middle of a fucking storm.

"Good work out there, Gael," Drake said.

"The scar's not going to be pretty." Gael looked down at his hands. "I'm really not cut out to be a surgeon."

"He'll be alive to tell the story, which is more than would have happened if you hadn't been there."

"We're home," the pilot informed them. Moments later, they felt the helicopter touch the ground gently. They moved quickly out of the way, making space for the two doctors who jumped inside to help with the patient. Jens exchanged a couple words with one of the two women, and then moved to the side, letting them take over.

As they stepped out of the helicopter, it had finally stopped raining.

"*Cerveza*?" Gael suggested, smiling.

"What a day," Drake said. "You guys all—"

The words died in his mouth as Jens's large body crumpled. Drake rushed forward, only just managing to catch his friend before he hit the tarmac.

"I need help here!" Drake shouted.

10

Isolde

This wasn't the first time Isolde had rushed to the hospital in the middle of the night. In her line of work, it happened more often than she'd like, such as whenever a police officer was injured—but getting a call from Drake, asking him to meet him at the hospital, had terrified her.

He called me.

That means he's okay.

It has to mean that.

Putting on the same clothes she'd worn to work earlier that day, which were still lying across the back of a chair, Isolde got into her car and drove to the Hôpital du Pays in record time. She was glad there was still no snow on the roads.

I really have to get rid of that car sometime …

She hadn't thought of asking Drake where he was, but assumed the Urgences desk was the most reasonable place to start looking. She knew a lot of people here, but not the two women manning the reception.

She was about to approach them when she suddenly saw Drake, pacing at the end of the corridor, outside the restricted area.

"Drake!"

Physically, he seemed to be okay. He was wearing navy blue technical pants and a light blue polo shirt, covered in stains.

Is that blood?

His expression, as he looked up at her, was so bleak, that for a moment she wasn't sure what to do. Then her instinct kicked in—she ran towards him and wrapped her arms tightly around him.

It wasn't quite the comforting embrace she would have wanted to provide, since she only came to his shoulders, but he leaned down and returned it.

"Thank you for coming. I'm sorry I called. I shouldn't have—"

"Of course you should have. Are you okay?" she asked, running her hand along his back and arms.

"Me? I'm fine," he said. He inhaled sharply. "But I could have killed half of my team today, Isolde."

"What happened?" she asked. His skin had a level of pallor to it she'd never seen before.

"We were sent out to rescue a climber. Gael went down first. The storm was raging, and then Jens—"

His voice broke into a strangled sob.

For a moment she feared the worst. But Drake wouldn't have been standing outside the restricted emergency area if—

"Is he going to be okay?"

Drake nodded. "It looks like it, but he could have died. It's only because Kat is such a fucking amazing pilot that Jens is still alive."

Drake turned towards the wall. Isolde knew he was considering putting a dent in the wall with his fist.

"Punching that wall is probably the easiest way to get yourself kicked out of the hospital, Drake," she said gently, taking his large hand in hers.

"Remember what you said to me, Doc? About the failed hero complex?"

She nodded, not liking where he was going with this.

"You're taking it out of context, Drake. What I was trying to say is that you can't save everyone. Failing to save someone is not failing them, Drake."

"Fuck. I don't know what I'm saying. I didn't call you here because I needed your professional help. I just wanted to—"

Isolde drove her body tighter against his.

"I understand."

As each and every time they touched, the feeling was electric. Her curves and his hard lines simply fit together.

"Hey, Isolde," Kat said, strolling towards them.

Isolde broke the hug, taking a step back from Drake. She didn't know what Kat would think to see them like this, but Kat didn't look surprised or particularly curious.

Isolde and Kat weren't close friends, but they were two women in a largely male office, so they had crossed paths before.

"Kat. I hear you did some pretty incredible flying today."

"Is that what he told you?" Isolde said, taking a sip of her coffee and grimacing. "I don't understand why hospitals have to serve such dreadful coffee. It's like adding insult to injury, literally."

She placed the cup gently on one of the plastic seats behind her. "Did he also tell you I clipped the wall? Almost single-handedly destroying a three hundred thousand euro machine?"

Isolde smiled at Kat's attempt to lighten the tone.

"How did Jens get hurt?"

"While I was trying to get control of the helicopter, Drake winched him back into the machine. He hit his head as he was being dragged in, but he never said anything—just continued working until he collapsed as we got back into town."

Isolde shook her head.

"It looks like you all did pretty much everything right." Her eyes shifted to Drake. He clearly wasn't buying that message.

"It would have been deadly if Kat hadn't been such a great pilot."

"It seems this great pilot miscalculated her chances of getting Jens onto that ledge safely."

"I was the one who told you to do it. It was *my* call."

And there was the heart of the problem. Drake felt responsible.

"I should have taken more care with the weather. I should have found another way to get to that climber, that didn't involve risking yours or Jens's life."

Isolde noted Drake said nothing about his own life. She straightened up, about to reply in a calm, professional voice, when Kat took a step forward. Her voice, when she spoke, was shrill.

"You don't get to do this, Drake. You don't get to do this to me, and you don't get to do it to Jens, either. We did our job. We've all been trained, and we all understand the risk we take every day. It's our fucking job—the one we've chosen. And we work together, we make all these decisions together. You're not a lone ranger, Drake. This weight isn't one you get to take on your thick shoulders. So don't be stupid."

Drake stared at Kat, his mouth open in surprise. Isolde noted he wasn't denying anything Kat had said.

"You going to start on me as well?" Drake asked sullenly, looking at Isolde.

She put her palms up. "No, I think she said everything I could have hoped to say to you right now." She paused for a moment. "You should both go home and get some sleep. You look dead on your feet."

Drake squared his shoulders, as if ready for a fight.

"I'm not leaving until we see Jens."

Kat met Isolde's gaze held on. The pilot shrugged her slim shoulders.

"Then we stay," Isolde said, sitting down to wait on one of the hard, plastic chairs.

11

Drake

The next morning, Drake paced up and down the hospital corridor, waiting for Jens to be released. Once he'd been sure that was going to happen, Drake had gone home to take a shower and get changed, then come back to the hospital.

He wanted to be the one to pick Jens up and apologize—not for him getting hurt, but for not checking up on him afterwards, the way team members are supposed to do for one another.

Drake looked up. From the annoyed glance the reception area nurse was giving him, she wasn't taking kindly to his pacing.

In the early morning light, it was easy to see that he'd been wrong the night before—caught in guilt and panic of his own making. He almost chuckled, thinking about how the two women had reamed him a new one, standing right here in this very corridor.

They'd been right, and he'd been wrong. Just like he'd never thought of blaming anybody else in the team when he'd been injured, it was unfair and presumptuous of him to believe that Kat and Jens would feel any different.

Need to keep that failed hero complex in check.

His phone rang. He got another cold look from the nurse—he'd forgotten to turn the ringer off.

"Drake? It's Hugo."

"Hugo. How are you?"

"Good. Listen, just wanted to update you on the investigation. We've been looking into the possibility of a technical malfunction, but haven't had any luck so far. It just doesn't seem to make any sense.

"Sorry to hear that."

"But at least the two guys are doing okay. One's been discharged from the hospital already, the other one will probably get out this week. They were lucky you were there."

"Yeah. That's good to hear. Thanks for the update, Hugo. Let me know if I can help with anything."

Drake stood up to see Jens being wheeled out by a pretty brunette nurse. The sight of the wheelchair made him want to throw up.

"Relax, Drake, it's just hospital policy," Jens said good-naturedly. The nurse accompanied them all the way to the exit, where Jens said goodbye to her as if they'd known each other their whole lives.

"Dude, here I was, worried about you, and you were—"

"Get your mind out of the gutter, Drake. I was just being friendly."

"Are you sure you're okay to walk to the car? Did the doctor say—"

"I'm a doctor, Drake."

Drake frowned. "You were a doctor yesterday as well, if I'm not mistaken, when you ignored all symptoms of a concussion and crumpled on the ground."

"I didn't crumple on the ground. It appears you caught me."

"I should have let you fall."

"What the hell are you doing here, anyway?" Jens asked. Despite his brave words, he walked slower than usual. Drake kept pace with him, not wanting to rush him.

"I thought I'd come over and take you home. I wanted to—"

"Careful with what you're going to say next, Drake. You're my friend, and I don't want to have to deck you, but if you try to take responsibility for this—"

Drake nodded. "No. I tried that last night. Isolde and Kat set me straight."

"Isolde was here, huh," Jens said. His warm brown eyes crinkled at the corners.

"I called her," Drake confessed.

"Good for you, man, good for you."

Drake pressed the key fob and opened the car. He debated whether to walk over to the passenger seat and help Jens, then decided against it. Moving slowly, his friend got in the car.

"I wanted to say sorry for not realizing that you were hurt, Jens."

Jens shrugged lightly. Drake didn't miss the wince that crossed his friend's face before he schooled it back into a neutral expression. "It was my fault more than anything else. I should have told you I was dizzy, but I thought ice and an aspirin would fix it."

"How bad *is* it?" Drake asked.

"Grade 2 concussion. I'll take the day off today and be fine tomorrow."

"Tomorrow? You're sure? Maybe I should speak with your doctor."

"Jesus, Drake, take me home, please. You're worse than Damien, and that's saying something."

Drake's phone rang.

"Speak of the Devil, it's Damien. Damien, how are you?"

"Drake! Are you okay? How's Jens?" There was an edge to his voice.

He's already heard.

Drake put his friend and boss on speaker phone.

"Everything's fine, Damien," Jens said. "Small concussion. Nothing to worry about."

"I thought you weren't back until next week," Drake said.

"We're still in Sardinia. I got a call from Beau this morning."

"The snitch."

"You should have called me."

"Nothing to worry about, Commandant. Kat, Jens and I are fine. How's Tess? How's Sardinia?"

"She's doing well. Thinking about Jamie constantly, though. Maybe we should have brought him out here with us."

Drake chuckled. It didn't surprise him in the least. His friend Damien had been lucky to find a woman who happened to love his son Jamie as much as she loved Damien. And Jamie loved her right back.

"Tell her Jamie's doing well. Your father is spoiling him like crazy. And I'll be taking him bouldering next weekend."

"Go to the beach, Damien. Enjoy your time off with your bride," Jens said, resting his head against the car seat.

Drake realized he hadn't been to the beach in years. He had to admit the thought of Isolde in a bathing suit made him want to plan a long weekend away. Maybe he could convince her—

Jens chuckled again, and Drake realized he'd missed part of the conversation.

"We'll be glad to have you back next week, Commandant," Jens said.

"Call me if you need anything, please. I can get back sooner."

They spent a couple more minutes reassuring their boss. By the time they hung up the call, both Drake and Jens were smiling.

12

Drake

That evening, Drake had gone to see Isolde, bringing takeaway from a local Asian fusion restaurant.

He'd told himself he wanted to thank her for coming to the hospital to see him in the middle of the night—but he knew he was kidding himself, he'd just needed to see her.

She'd been so impressed to see he'd guessed her favorite restaurant, he almost didn't want to mention he'd seen the magnet on her fridge door the first time he'd been up to her apartment.

They'd skipped dessert and had sex together instead. Amazing sex. The kind he couldn't even have described to anyone, not that he was the kind of man to kiss and tell.

Isolde hadn't exactly asked him to stay afterwards but hadn't kicked him out either, and they'd even had a cup of coffee together before he'd run off home to get changed before going into the office.

They'd agreed to meet again on Wednesday, but this time he hadn't been sure what to bring. He was a half-decent cook, and thought maybe Isolde would enjoy a home-cooked meal. He'd checked her fridge that morning before he left and found it empty save for some old milk and a piece of Parmesan cheese, so he'd stopped by the Sherpa Supermarket after work.

Even with that stop, he'd made it to her place before her. He had always thought he and his team worked hard, but he was now discovering just how hard Isolde worked. She was one of the first people in the office in the mornings, and rarely came home before eight at night.

Drake stayed in his car until he saw her ratty little Golf shuffling up the street. While she parked, he got out with his armful of groceries. Suddenly, he felt shy.

Am I acting like a pest?

The kind of guest she simply can't get rid of?

Then he saw her smile as she caught sight of him. It lit up her expression, turning her from pretty to blindingly beautiful in the space of a millisecond. She walked towards him in those serious-looking heels. He loved the way her hips swayed as she walked in them.

Maybe we should leave the heels on tonight.

"Hey," he said. He leaned down to give her a quick kiss, but she looked up at the same time. Their cheeks collided.

"Sorry," they both said at the same time.

"I thought we could cook tonight." He hesitated for a moment. "If you're not busy."

"I was going to call you," she breathed. "As soon as I'd taken off my heels." She grimaced. Suddenly, he didn't like those shoes nearly as much.

"What did you bring?" She went up on tiptoes, trying to see into the bags in his arms. He raised his arms and kept the bags out of her reach, laughing.

"You'll see, sweetheart, you'll see." The endearment rolled off his tongue before he could think better of it. Sweetheart. He'd never used an endearment with another woman before. But it fit Isolde.

She paused for a second by the door. She'd noticed as well. He waited for her to react, but she didn't say anything. He debated whether to ask her about it later. For now, he wanted to feed her.

Upstairs in her apartment, Drake took off his shoes at the entrance and carried the bags to her small kitchen, which took up one corner of the living room.

Thank goodness I brought everything I need for tonight's meal.

"It doesn't look like you cook much," he said, opening and closing a couple cabinets. "What do you normally eat?"

It was hard to think of a normal which didn't include him, but Isolde was a grown woman—she'd been feeding herself for years.

She shrugged. "Wine and cheese, sometimes. Or else, I order something in."

She'd taken off her suit jacket and the offending heels and was now standing by the small kitchen island which doubled as an informal breakfast table. With her hand, she rubbed each of her small feet, in turn, groaning.

Drake felt like groaning himself.

If she keeps that up, I'll forget all about dinner.

He shook himself. No. She'd been working all day, and he wanted to make her a nice meal. He wanted to get to know her better. And a part of him also didn't want her to think he came only for—

"So, what are we eating? How can I help?"

He took a long time to answer, as if trying to decide what exactly he could task her with. Finally, she laughed out loud. He loved the sound of her laugh.

"I said I didn't cook much, Drake, not that I won't know what to do with myself in a kitchen. I can follow instructions."

He felt himself grow harder. He could give her instructions to follow.

The meal, Drake. She means the meal.

He shrugged lightly and fought the urge to rearrange himself. He was a grown man, not a horny teenager.

"We're making a lettuce, avocado, apple and pine nut salad. How about you start by washing some lettuce, and we go from there?"

She laughed again, a musical sound. "I get the feeling you don't really trust me." But she moved closer to him and picked up the lettuce, taking it to the sink. In her bare feet, she barely came to his collarbone.

I trust you, Isolde.

More than you can imagine.

"I trust you," he said. He wasn't talking about the salad anymore, but he tried to keep his tone of voice light—no point in making her feel uncomfortable.

Soon they were working together side by side.

This is better than takeout.

When the food was ready, they set a couple place-mats on the kitchen island. He sliced the fresh, country bread. As he served the salad, Isolde sipped her red wine delicately. Her small tongue came out to lick her lips, and he thought he might explode.

"Stop doing that, please," he begged.

Her eyes widened—she really did not know what he was speaking about. He pointed to the wine glass, then his thumb went to her lips, rubbing gently against the top, then the bottom lip.

She groaned. "You're the one who needs to stop that."

"What if I don't want to stop?" he whispered.

Her eyes went to his trousers. It was getting harder and harder to hide his interest.

Her small hands went to his belt, undoing it quickly and efficiently. His fork froze on the way to his mouth.

"I wanted to feed you," he said.

"I'm not hungry for food," she replied.

Her hand went down the front of his pants, grabbing on to his erection through his boxer shorts. It was all he could do to stand still and breathe in deeply, hoping he wouldn't blow his load. Then she started rubbing softly through the cotton.

"I guess you did miss me today," she said. As she touched him, her honey eyes held his gaze.

He wanted nothing but to put her up on the table and feast on her as his meal.

"Let me show you just how much I missed you."

She was still wearing those sexy black pants, paired with a long-sleeved white blouse. Too many clothes. He undid the buttons of her pants carefully, letting the fabric slide down her hips until it pooled on the floor around her feet.

Drake stared at the wispy white lace covering her hips and ass. He could smell her through the panties, a smell both earthy and fresh at the same time.

"Your panties drive me insane," he whispered against her ear. "All day I've been wondering what color they were ..."

"Now you know," she whispered.

Those need to come off.

He hooked his thumb into the waistline and

pulled them down her legs until they joined her suit pants.

Drake didn't give her time to step out of them. He picked Isolde up and lifted her bodily onto the side of the table that was clear of plates. His large hands went on either side of her knees, spreading her legs.

"What are you doing, Drake?" she asked, uncertainly.

"Feasting." He opened her legs further, revealing her beautiful pink folds.

"Turn the lights off," she said. Her knees fought against his hands but he held her open to his view.

"I'm not turning the lights off. I want to see how many orgasms I can lick out of this pretty pink pussy."

Her breath hitched. She was getting hot from dirty talk. He lowered himself to his knees and brought his tongue to her folds. She tasted like coming home.

She jumped up. "I should take a shower first—"

"Later," he growled. He kept his touch light. He hadn't shaved since that morning, and didn't want to hurt her sensitive skin. His tongue made its way up and down her slit until it finally uncovered her clit. The little button jumped under his touch.

Isolde moaned, arching against him. He should have taken off the blouse so he could see her breasts.

Next time.

She'd stopped fighting him. Now, one of her hands threaded in his hair, pushing him against her.

Exactly where I want to be.

"More," she begged. "More."

Happy to oblige, Drake licked and sucked, bringing her higher and higher, until she finally exploded, bucking into his mouth. Next to his face, her calves stretched beautifully, her toes pointing downwards.

He kept licking gently, wanting to wring out the full pleasure out of her orgasm.

Finally, she collapsed, and would have fallen back onto the hard surface if he hadn't held her upright.

"I've got you," he said.

"You certainly do. That was—" And then his mouth was on her. It turned him on to know she'd be able to taste herself in his kiss.

Drake was hard as a rock under his technical pants. He wanted to be inside her. But he wanted to see all of her first.

Still supporting her with one hand, he used his other hand to undo the buttons on her blouse until he could slide it off her shoulders. This time he didn't stop to admire the lacy bra—he wanted a look at what was underneath. He unhooked it quickly, tossing it behind them.

Her breasts were magnificent—as amazing as he remembered them, but even better now that he could see them properly. He was never turning the lights off again. Her nipples pebbled under his gaze.

He looked into Isolde's eyes and caught the uncertainty in her gaze. She no longer looked as sated and relaxed as she had been just seconds earlier.

"My breasts are—"

"Fucking perfect," he finished for her.

She shrugged gently, but something was still concerning her.

"What's wrong, Isolde? Tell me."

"You're too dressed," she said.

If that's what's bothering her, I can fix that.

Drake took off his polo shirt quickly. His belt buckle was already undone, so he made quick work of pulling off his pants and boxer shorts. In an instant, he was standing naked in front of her.

"I want to make you come again," he said. His finger went to her folds, finding her wet for him.

"Together," she whispered. Her hand wrapped itself against her cock. Drake shook. He wasn't going to make it very far like that.

Thankfully he'd remembered to take a condom from his pocket—he rolled it off quickly and matter-of-factly on his cock, enjoying the way she watched.

He lifted her easily onto his hips, holding on to her ass with his hands. His eyes targeted on the empty wall in front of them—he was going to take her against the wall and—

Suddenly, he realized she was squirming in his arms.

"Put me down," she said. "I'm too heavy."

Drake stopped where he was.

Fuck the wall.

He'd show her he didn't need the wall for what he wanted to do to her.

"No," he said.

He'd never found a better use for his strength than this. Looking straight into her eyes, he lifted her higher up. He lined her right against his cock and slowly—ever so slowly—pushed her down onto his erection.

She gasped, and her body tensed at the intrusion. He gave her time to adjust until she started moving against him.

"You okay?" he said.

"Mmmm ... I want more."

More he could do. Drake lifted her gently up and down on his cock, the connection so intense he had to slow down or stop several times.

"More," she demanded.

"If I give you more, I'll come."

Her pussy muscles clenched against him. She seemed to like that thought.

"Stop that, Isolde. I mean it. Or I'll have to leave you."

Her eyebrows came up in alarm. "If you leave, I'll kill you."

He laughed. "Okay. Then stay still. But let me catch my breath."

But there was no catching his breath like this. Her pussy was tight—even through the condom, he felt how his cock *filled* her. His hands spread out on her ass, enjoying the feeling of her curves against his hands. He realized he wasn't going to be last long, and the last thing he wanted to do was leave her wanting.

He increased the tempo, lifting her and lowering her onto his cock, watching as the blush spread on her cheeks and around her collarbone.

"Drake, I'm going to come," she said breathlessly.

"Yes. Come on my cock, Isolde. Come on my cock now."

And then she did. Her muscles clenched against him, milking his own orgasm out of her. He came on a roar, holding her tight against him.

For the first time in his life, he wished he weren't wearing a condom. He wanted to flood her with his come and—

Drake shut that thought up quickly, not knowing where it'd come from. He'd never, ever had sex without a condom before—nor had he ever wanted to.

Her body sagged against his, her cheek coming to rest on his shoulder, her arms around his neck.

The pleasure was so strong, his legs suddenly felt unsteady. He needed a bed. He turned and walked quickly towards her bedroom. As he approached the bed, he lifted Isolde off his softening cock, careful to hold on to the condom with his other hand, and lay her on the bed.

He disposed of the condom quickly in the bathroom and came back. Isolde was still sprawled on the bed where he'd left her.

"Make space for me, sleepy head," he said in a hushed voice.

She opened an eye. "Where are we?"

"In bed."

She nodded. "That was the best orgasm of my life, Drake." Moments later, she was asleep. Drake curled his body around hers and covered them with her light duvet.

His last thought, before falling asleep beside her, was that they'd never finished the meal.

13

Isolde

I solde woke up starving, her stomach rumbling like she hadn't eaten in a day.

Which makes sense since we skipped dinner.

She thought of the meal she and Drake had so painstakingly prepared—then blushed as she remembered how they'd barely had a bite before they ended up in each other's arms.

In each other's arms.

She almost giggled. The euphemism wasn't enough to explain what it'd felt like, to be lifted again and again onto his cock while looking straight into his beautiful gray eyes. Not that she'd ever doubted Drake's strength, but that had been badass.

Mind-blowing.

She turned over to look at him. He was lying on his side, snoring softly with an arm over his eyes. Like her, he was naked. She ran her eyes down his sleeping form, from his muscled upper chest to his slim hips—then the hard lines of his butt and legs, currently covered by the duvet.

She wondered if he woke up with a hard-on—the morning hard-on was something she'd read about consistently, but her experience with men was too limited to know if it was true. Certainly her last long-term boyfriend, a lawyer called Olivier, had woken up with what she'd referred to in her mind as a *smartphone hard-on*. He'd started reading his emails on his way to the shower, and disappeared into his work world long before he'd left for work.

Probably goes a long way to explain why it didn't work out for us.

She couldn't imagine Drake waking up and choosing his phone over her, unless he received an emergency call.

Isolde was tempted to lift the duvet and check—if he was hard, maybe they'd have time to do something about it.

She looked at her phone to confirm the time—and froze, staring at the dark screen, her hand still on the side button. It wasn't the time—06:20—but rather the date, that had her heart almost stopping.

It was the one-year anniversary of the day her patient had killed himself. Pierre Omont had been a twenty-nine-year-old Chamonix gendarme. He'd had a stellar track record and his whole life ahead of him. And then—

Isolde's eyes filled with tears.

"Isolde? Is everything okay?"

Isolde looked back to find Drake sitting up in bed, looking at her. His eyes were full of concern.

No. Nothing is okay.

"I'm okay," she said mechanically. It wasn't like Drake could do anything to help. "I'm sorry, but I need to be alone."

Drake pulled on his boxer shorts and pants in one quick move.

"Please, Isolde. Tell me what's going on. You're scaring me."

"I'm okay. I just ... I didn't realize that today I needed ... it's been great spending time with you over the last few days, Drake, but I need some time, okay?"

She saw by the widening of his gray eyes how much she was hurting him. He quickly finished putting on his clothes—a detached part of her thought it should be a crime to cover that body—then stood in front of her. She had to crane her neck up to see him.

"Please don't do this, Isolde. Don't lock me out. We did this to each other years ago, and I don't think I can do it again. Whatever's wrong, you can tell me."

It was a long speech by Drake's standards—there it was, his heart, out there for her to see. But Isolde couldn't deal with it, not today. She still couldn't believe she'd forgotten what day it was today.

What if I'm so distracted I lose track of the next Pierre?

"I'm sorry, Drake," she said lamely. "I told you I didn't want a relationship. If you misunderstood—"

He clenched his square jaw. "I don't need a label for what we have together, Isolde, but I also don't expect to be kicked to the curb in the mornings."

He was right, of course. There was nothing she could say to that.

Drake sighed. "I'll get out of your way, Isolde. But please believe me when I say, we can be so much more than *that*," he said, pointing towards the bed behind them, "if you'll let me in."

A moment later, his black boots were on and he was out of the door.

I'm sorry, Drake.

She'd hurt him—and hurt herself as well. Because, regardless of what she'd told him, this wasn't just about sex for her. It'd never been about sex.

Isolde showered and dressed quickly, still feeling the weight of the world on her shoulders.

At seven a.m., as she was getting ready to go out, her doorbell rang. Her heart fluttered.

Drake.

He'd come back for her. He'd—

It wasn't Drake standing outside, but a slim, pale brunette in her mid-twenties. Although large sunglasses obscured half her face, and even though it'd been almost a year since she'd last seen her, Isolde had no trouble recognizing her.

Amélie Omont.

Drake

All morning, Drake had kept thoughts of Isolde at bay through sheer force of will alone. His wasn't a job where he could afford that kind of distraction, so his wounded heart would have to wait until the evening.

Thankfully, he'd been kept busy. He and his team had been out twice that morning already, first to rescue a family of walkers who had overestimated their seven-year-old twins' stamina and found themselves stuck on the steep slopes of the Combe Noire, then to rescue a thirty-year-old climber who'd injured her elbow following an accidental fall. The woman had been a good sport, but that injury had to have hurt.

Sitting at his desk now, Drake rubbed at his leg absentmindedly. He was smart enough to recognize the phantom pain for what it was.

"I'm hungry," Gael said.

"You're always hungry," Kat replied good naturedly.

"Not my fault if I've got an active metabolism," Gael said, patting his flat belly.

"We don't need to hear about your metabolism, Gael. Though I do think I could eat. Jens?"

The doctor nodded, standing up. He was back at work, though Drake was keeping him on desk duty for a few days. The fact that Jens hadn't complained about that let him know it'd been the right choice.

Hiro and Bailey were at the vet for a check-up, so they wouldn't be back until later that day.

"Sure," Drake said, standing up as well. "Let's go grab something."

At that moment, Isolde walked out of the elevator. Drake's heart missed a beat.

What is she doing down here?

Her eyes took in the surrounding room, until they landed on him. She paused uncertainly, then started walking towards him.

"Uh, hi Kat, Gael. How are you feeling, Jens?"

"Good, good. Thanks for asking, Isolde."

"I ... uh ... was wondering if we could speak for a minute, Drake."

Drake nodded. He was unable to take his gaze off her.

"See you later, Drake," Jens said, neatly stepping away from him. Kat and Gael waved as well. Moments later, the two of them were alone in their side of the office.

"Is everything okay, Isolde?" He was having trouble interpreting the nervous energy coming from her. She didn't look as bleak as she had earlier that morning, when she'd all but kicked him out of her place, but she also didn't look *okay*.

"I owe you an apology for this morning," she began.

"I don't need an apology, Isolde." Drake replied impatiently. "I just need to know you're okay."

"Last night made me forget what today was. When I woke up and saw the date—"

Drake kept silent, waiting for her to go on.

"Twelve months ago today, a man killed himself in the mountains. You might have heard of him—Sergeant Pierre Omont."

Fuck.

Of course Drake had heard of Pierre Omont. The man had been a young sergeant who, after training for almost three years to join the PGHM, had developed migraines and severe vertigo, which had stopped him from passing the tests.

Drake searched in his memory for the man's death. It hadn't been his team who recovered the body, but he'd been present at the funeral, along with most of the Chamonix and Annecy police departments.

Isolde's eyes filled with tears. Drake clenched his hands to stop himself from wiping at her cheeks. It didn't look like she wanted to be touched.

"Did you know him well?" he asked gently. And then it all clicked in his mind. "You were his psychologist, weren't you?"

She nodded. "The last time we met, I got the feeling he was coming to terms with the change in his circumstances. He wasn't going to join the PGHM. But he was married, he seemed happy. I didn't think he would ..."

She sobbed. Drake couldn't help himself anymore. He crossed the distance between them and drew her into his arms.

A moment later, she stepped back. He wished her eyes didn't look so bleak.

"I need your help, Drake," she said.

"Anything." He meant it, too.

"I need to go up to Bossons. To where Pierre jumped."

Drake waited for her to go on.

"As I said, Pierre was married. His widow came to see me. She's ... she's not having an easy time. I'd like to go up there with her. I think it will help her. I *hope* it will help her get closure, so she can move on."

Drake didn't push her. A part of him was elated that Isolde had come to him. "What do you have in mind?" he asked.

14

Drake

"Thanks for doing this, Kat," Drake said. Although he was sitting right next to her in the cockpit, both of them were wearing headsets to protect their hearing. "I owe you one."

"No problem, Drake. What are days off for, if not to help a friend?"

She didn't say this was the first time they were taking a helicopter out for personal reasons. She didn't need to say so, just like he didn't need to tell her that, should anybody ask, he would take full responsibility.

Drake turned his head to look at Isolde and Amélie Omont, the two passengers in the back of the helicopter.

"You think this is a good idea?"

She shrugged. "I don't know. Isolde seems to think so. And if it were me ... I think I would want closure as well."

Drake nodded. "You're probably right. I can't imagine what that poor woman is going through."

Isolde had wanted to bring Amélie Omont up to the Bossons Glacier, to the place where investigators thought her husband jumped, but she hadn't wanted to spend the day hiking and extend the young widow's misery—hence where he and Kat came in.

"You think you'll be able to put us down at the top?" he said, looking at his map on the tablet in front of him.

Kat nodded easily. "I know the area. It'll be a quick hike to where—to where it happened."

It was difficult to know the exact spot Sergeant Omont had jumped from, but police investigators had been able to narrow it down to a specific path on a ridge near the glacier. It was a practicable path, but if somebody fell—or jumped—on the steep side of it, it was a good four hundred meter fall to the bottom.

More than enough for someone looking to end it all.

It also didn't matter if it wasn't exactly the right place.

It's still closure.

Drake looked at his two passengers. Isolde had changed into technical pants not much different from the ones he wore—except they fit her a lot better—and a pair of used hiking boots.

Amélie Omont was wearing jeans that looked too tight for hiking, but at least she was also wearing a pair of good boots on her feet. Isolde had told him Amélie was a teller in one of the local banks. Drake wondered what the last year had been like for the widow.

Is this the first time she's coming back to the mountains that claimed her husband's life?

Drake hadn't spent any time thinking about her this last year. He wondered if anyone, other than Isolde, had been in touch with her.

That didn't mean Pierre Omont's team had forgotten him. But, in their line of work, sometimes there were casualties. Civilians, but also team members. And survivors had to make tough choices—they had to compartmentalize, in order to be able to keep doing their job.

Drake looked over at Kat. Her lips were pursed in concentration. He wondered if she also was having similar thoughts.

Eventually, Drake made his way to the back of the helicopter.

"We're going to be landing in a couple minutes. Make sure you're strapped in," he added unnecessarily. Neither woman had moved since they first sat down.

Drake exchanged a quick look with Isolde. Her eyes were bright with sadness.

This is really hard for her.

He wanted to hold her and lend her some of his

strength. He might not have much else to offer, but he was strong. She could lean on him. Always.

But now wasn't the right time. She'd asked for his help getting to the ridge. He was certainly not going to leave her and Amélie Omont alone up here, but he wouldn't get in their way. Isolde had a plan, and Drake would support her in making it happen.

Kat landed the helicopter softly and without fanfare, and they all jumped out.

Often during an extraction, Kat stayed with the helicopter, ready to fly out as soon as the team was back with the rescues. This time, however, was different. Any chance to rescue someone had come and gone over a year earlier. Today was just about closure. Kat locked the helicopter and all four of them stepped out onto the path together.

Isolde and Amélie walked up front, talking gently. Drake and Kat followed. He could hear bits of the conversation upfront.

"My heart hurts," Amélie confided in Isolde. Drake felt like he was snooping, but he couldn't stop himself from listening in. "He left me behind."

Isolde's soft voice carried towards him in the silence of the mountain. "We don't talk about this enough. The duty to protect is so engrained in police officers ... sometimes it overrides everything else. Pierre probably thought he was protecting you."

Drake swallowed—the phantom pain in his leg flared up again.

"We're here," he finally said. He'd spoken to the

commander in charge of the search, and was pretty certain they were standing in the right place.

"Some days, I think everything's going to be okay. Then the cloud comes back."

"I'm sorry, Amélie," Isolde said. "There's nothing any of us can say, but I know how much he cared about you. He told me often enough during our sessions together. He wouldn't have wanted you to be sad."

Amélie's shoulders slumped. "He shouldn't have left me. If I'd known—"

"This isn't on you, Amélie. It's on all of us," Isolde replied.

Drake bristled at the guilt hidden in Isolde's voice and bit his lip to avoid speaking his mind. Pierre had decided to take his own life. And as much as Drake wished the man had reached out to somebody beforehand, his failure to do so didn't transfer the blame onto Isolde's shoulders.

But Drake wouldn't—couldn't—judge the man's actions. Even at his lowest, after the cable car accident that had taken the girl's life and shattered his leg, Drake had never touched that rock bottom where taking his life might have seemed the preferable way forward. The fact that he'd never contemplated that had nothing to do with his own strength of character, and everything to do with his team, who'd stood by him and supported him until he'd regained his strength.

But he wouldn't judge Pierre's choices, however much devastation he'd left behind.

Beside him, Kat's hands were clenched into fists. Her red curls fell onto her face but she made no attempt to pull them back.

"It's peaceful here," Amélie finally breathed. Tears rolled down her face. "Thank you for bringing me. Before, I couldn't picture—" She stifled a sob.

Isolde gently brought Amélie back from the edge and helped her sit on a large, flat rock along the path. Isolde whispered something to Amélie, then moved a respectful distance away and sat on an overturned log. Drake and Kat followed. He made sure to take the spot on the log next to Isolde. He needed that connection.

Isolde's shoulders hunched. Drake couldn't bear to see her taking on all this weight herself. This wasn't the time or place to speak about it, but he sat as close to her as possible, his leg pressed up against hers. As time passed, and the air around them grew colder, all Drake could feel was the warm spot where their bodies touched.

15

Isolde

I solde wished she could say that closure for Amélie Omont had meant closure for her as well. It hadn't.

The truth was, Amélie Omont had been right. Somebody *should* have noticed Pierre was so close to breaking. And that somebody was Isolde.

Isolde was too smart to think that Pierre's decision had been anything but his own. And yet, she'd been the one treating him. She'd believed—and after his suicide had gone through her notes more times than she could count to remind herself of what she'd thought at each moment in time—that he was learning to cope with his emotions and moving in a positive direction now that his dream of joining the PGHM had been shattered.

But a day before their next scheduled meeting, Pierre had gone up to the Bossons—and never come home.

All these questions came rushing to her again now, as they had that very first day, standing in the Chamonix morgue.

What did I do wrong?

How could I miss this?

There was no obvious answer. No closure to be had. As a psychologist, as a professional, she knew her feelings of guilt and grief were natural, and that going on with her work was the best way to deal with them.

But it's hard.

And something else was bothering her. In the two days since the helicopter up to the Bossons, Drake hadn't called her nor come to see her.

She knew she was being unreasonable. There were any number of reasons why this could be the case. He might be busy with his job. He might be confused after her hot-cold-hot behavior. He might need some time alone. All completely valid reasons. And yet, here she was, pining away.

She opened her fridge, as if it might magically have filled itself in her absence, but of course it was still shockingly empty. She made a mental note to stop by the Sherpa store the next day—maybe get herself some fruit and vegetables.

For tonight, she was going to order in. She shuffled the take-away menus on her counter.

Sushi it is.

Less than twenty minutes later, her doorbell rang. Chamonix was a small town.

She buzzed the delivery person in without bothering to ask who it was and moved to wait by the open door. In her hand she held her card and a five euro note—she'd delivered pizzas while studying at university, and knew it took several great tips to make up for the number of people who didn't tip at all.

Isolde's mouth fell open as Drake stepped out of the elevator, a small bag from the sushi shop hanging from his arm.

"What are you doing here?"

"I brought your food."

"How—"

"I paid the young woman and told her I'd bring it up."

Isolde frowned. "And she believed you? How did she know you weren't just going to steal my sushi?"

"What can I say? I look trustworthy," Drake laughed, handing over her bag. "I also tipped her generously, enough for her to risk getting a call from a hungry, angry customer."

Isolde smiled. "You should probably come inside, though I'm not sure I ordered enough for both of us."

"I'm not hungry," Drake said, just as his stomach rumbled. He had the grace to look sheepish. "Okay, maybe a bit hungry. But I know there's nothing in our fridge except ketchup and maybe some old cheese, and really I just ... I wanted to see you."

Isolde closed the door behind them.

"I'm glad you came," she said. They were too old to dance around their feelings.

"I wanted to talk to you and see how you're doing. I could tell how hard the trip on the mountains was for you."

"I'm okay. I've been feeling a bit lost but I think ... no, I *know*, it's all going to be okay. How about you? You look tired."

"I'm sorry I didn't call. We had a couple busy days—didn't get much sleep last night, looking for a missing family of hikers."

That answers one question.

"Did you find them? Are they okay?" She wasn't sure she wanted to hear the answer.

He nodded. "They're okay. They'll probably buy better shoes before they try something like this again."

"I'm glad. I can't imagine how difficult it is, doing what you do, every day."

"No more difficult than what you do, Isolde. If anything, you're the one who ends up dealing with the fallout when things go south."

Drake sat down across from her at her dining table. Isolde couldn't help but think of the last time they'd stood here, how he'd lifted her in his arms and—

Drake's eyes heated up."Stop looking at me like

that, Isolde. I want to let you eat your dinner—but I'm only human."

Isolde hid a smile as she got up to find some chopsticks. As she handed him a pair, his fingers caught hold of her hand gently. It was all she could do to suppress a sigh as his touch seared her.

"Sit down, Isolde. Eat with me."

"I hope you like shrimp tempura, salmon and butter fish," she said.

He laughed, looking at the small spread before them. "It's very generous of you, to share this plentiful meal."

"I would have ordered more if you'd called ahead to tell me you were coming." Isolde pointed to her forehead. "I made a mental note to stop by the grocery store tomorrow on my way home."

"Why don't you come to my place for dinner tomorrow?"

"Your place?"

He nodded. "I have an apartment as well. Or did you think I slept in the office?"

She worried her lip with her teeth for a moment. It seemed like a big step.

"You live alone?"

"I do." He dropped his chopsticks. "Are you afraid somebody will see us?"

"Not afraid per se, but we ... we work together."

He nodded, his expression firm and determined. "We'll tell the colonel—"

"Hold your horses, Drake."

"Let me finish. You already filed a report claiming we shouldn't work together. I want to take it one step further. We'll tell the colonel we're seeing each other, that's all."

"You make it sound simple."

"It *is* simple, Isolde. I want to have sex with you all the fucking time. But I also want *more*."

"What if I'm not ready for more?"

"Then I'll wait until you're ready."

She nodded slowly. "I need to think about it, Drake."

"Take as long as you need. I'm not going anywhere."

He's not going anywhere.

Warmth pooled in her lower belly.

She pointed at the last piece of sushi but Drake leaned back, shaking his head. "Too full," he said, laughing. Isolde picked it up with her chopsticks, skillfully dipping the corner into the soy sauce before bringing it into her mouth. She closed her eyes as the flavors exploded in her mouth.

Drake

Drake groaned as Isolde chewed on what clearly must be her favorite maki roll.

He stood up and took her in his arms. Her hair smelled of something flowery and fresh, like her. He

136

worried he might be squeezing her too hard but, the moment he attempted to release her, she pulled him back.

"Hold on to me," she whispered.

"I'm not letting you go."

No matter what.

"Come to bed," she said, taking his hand in her smaller one.

For the first time in his life, he wished he had a different kind of job.

"Not tonight. I'm on duty again in an hour. I just needed to see you for first."

"Okay," she said. "Tomorrow is Saturday. How about we—"

Fuck.

"I can't. I have a date with Jamie—Damien's son. We're going bouldering."

Her lips stretched into a small smile. "You're still doing that."

He nodded. "He's less interested in me now that school has started again, but we go out once every few weeks." Then he had a sudden inspiration. "Why don't you join us?"

"Bouldering?" she asked, looking at herself. "I'm not sure my physique is really suited—"

"Two legs and two arms," Drake said. "That's all you need. And I've seen people boulder successfully with less than that."

"Easy for you to say, when you're made of muscle. Fine. Tomorrow afternoon it is."

"I'll pick you up at two."

Isolde

So that's how Isolde found herself stuck to a rock on a sunny Saturday afternoon. Or rather, attempting to stick to a rock. Like a limpet. Or a leech.

"I'm going to fall," Isolde said. And if fear colored her words, well, that was only to be expected.

Jamie laughed. "You're really close to the ground, Dr. Durant."

Isolde sneaked a look down—and blushed. In her mind she'd climbed much further, but she was still only a couple feet off the ground.

And there's a climbing mat right beneath you.

"Call me Isolde," she told the boy for the tenth time, speaking through gritted teeth.

To be fair, Jamie had been nothing but supportive all afternoon. The boy couldn't have been more excited to find someone who so clearly needed his help.

And Drake—Drake looked like he was enjoying himself tremendously.

He was wearing climbing shorts and a black T-shirt that wrapped itself around his abs and chest muscles. It didn't help that she knew exactly what was under the T-shirt. Flexing his powerful arms, he'd shown her the basics of bouldering as soon as they'd arrived—apparently there wasn't much technique involved, at least not at her level.

It was just a question of dragging herself up the wall and coming back down again.

Easier said than done.

Isolde thought self-consciously of her butt in the tight black leggings she was wearing, and of how large it must look to Drake, who stood right below her.

"You're overgripping, Isolde," Drake said calmly.

"What the hell does that even mean?" she groaned.

"It means you're clutching those holds with a death grip. Relax, the wall's not going anywhere."

Of course, him telling her to relax had exactly the opposite effect. If she'd been overgripping before, now she was about to crush the rock with her fingers.

Moments later, her fingers started cramping.

I'm going to fall.

"I'll catch you," Drake said.

Isolde hadn't even realized she'd spoken the thought out loud.

That's even worse. If I crush him, I'll never—

"Jump, Isolde, I promise I'll catch you."

She wasn't planning on jumping, but just then a fly landed on her left hand. She stupidly moved her right hand to swat it away—at least she was no longer overgripping—and ended up falling backwards.

Right into Drake's arms.

He caught her effortlessly, laughing.

Jamie clapped.

"It's my turn now, Uncle Drake!"

"You remember what I showed you last time?" Drake asked.

"I remember," the boy replied, looking up at the rock with a calculating expression on his little face.

No surprise, the boy was a much better climber than her. She watched him scale up the wall like a pro.

"That's high enough, Jamie. Come back down," Drake said sternly.

Jamie laughed, a sound full of happiness and joy. After what the boy had gone through just a couple months earlier, hearing him laugh like this—even if she was pretty sure he was laughing *at* her—was worth the trouble of coming up here.

"You did great, Jamie," Drake said. "Take a look at this picture I took."

In the picture, Jamie was high on the wall, looking for his next handhold. You could see him really thinking about his next move.

"Can we send it to my parents?"

"Of course," Drake said, and started typing away.

"They're coming back next week, you know?"

"I know."

"I've missed them a lot. Tess tells me they're going to bring me with them next time."

Drake laughed. "They've missed you too, little guy." He dug into his backpack for some snacks and water and passed them around.

He'll make an amazing dad.

Something heated inside her at the thought.

Are those my ovaries overgripping?

"You okay, Isolde?"

She almost choked on her water bottle, praying she hadn't spoken out loud.

"Fine. Just fine. It's pretty hot out here."

"Feel free to take something off," he whispered in her ear.

Isolde laughed and shook her head.

"Or not. I have a *really* good memory."

She realized she was having a wonderful time.

Finally, it was time to go home. The fifteen-minute hike from the car had seemed short hours earlier but now, her arms and legs shaking from the exertion, Isolde knew it was going to seem a lot longer.

While she struggled up a small hill, Drake walked easily up ahead. Jamie perched on his shoulders.

Lucky Jamie.

Isolde never thought she'd see the day when she was jealous of a six-year-old.

"Neither of you told me climbing was such—"

Suddenly, Drake was beside her. He kept one hand on Jamie's legs, but his other arm came out to stop her.

"What's wrong?" she asked.

He pointed ahead of them on the trail. For a moment she couldn't see anything. Then she heard it.

Something rustled behind the bushes—something large.

"Is that a *chamois*?" she asked, in a thin thread of voice. The chamois was a kind of large goat with small horns that curved backwards. Although rare in most of the world, chamois were a common enough occurrence all around the Mont Blanc massif—and only dangerous if you were a conifer tree.

But Drake wasn't staring at the bushes anymore—he was staring at the ground in front of them, a dark, foreboding expression on his face.

Putting his finger to his lips in the universal sign for silence, Drake took a step back, urging Isolde with him.

They'd only taken two steps back when the animal walked slowly out from behind the bushes.

Chamois, my ass.

They were staring into the green eyes of the largest cat Isolde had ever seen outside of a zoo.

Suddenly, those ten minutes separating them from the car might be ten light years away.

Not a chamois.

A lynx.

The sight of the solitary alpine predator filled her with a terror so thick she could taste it. As if aware of the effect she was having on Isolde, the large cat hissed, opening his powerful jaws to reveal sharp, white teeth.

"Fuck," Drake whispered. "Those climbers were right."

"Is that a lynx? I don't understand," Isolde said. "They don't attack—"

"From the prints on the ground, I think we're between her and her cub," Drake said, in a low voice.

That doesn't sound like good news.

The cat hissed as if in agreement, shifting elegantly to the side —Isolde and Drake moved as well, but the cat wasn't letting the distance between them grow.

The animal's body was lean and elegant, but there was no mistaking the strength in her jaws or the speed at which she could move.

In one slow, controlled movement, Drake brought Jamie down from his shoulders and placed him on the ground behind him. He then took a step forward, so he was standing in front of both Isolde and the boy.

"Isolde?"

Isolde nodded jerkily, taking her eyes away from the lynx.

"I'm going to need you to go back along the path the way we came. Keep Jamie in front of you at all times."

Bile inched up Isolde's throat.

"Are you crazy?" Now she was hissing as well. "I'm not leaving you here with *her.*"

Drake seemed to expect some pushback. He kept his eyes trained on the cat, who hissed at them again.

"The three of us are more at risk than I am on my

own," he said patiently. "I'm bigger. She won't know what to do with me."

Bullshit.

She looks like she knows exactly what to do with you.

"I need you to take Jamie away from here," Drake said, trying a different tack.

As if on queue, Jamie released a small, fearful sob. Isolde tightened her arms around his small body. Drake was right. They couldn't risk the boy.

Isolde nodded. "Okay. But I don't like this."

"Noted," Drake said. "Next time we meet a wild predator, we'll discuss a different strategy."

His eyes crinkled at the corner.

He's having fun.

Isolde took a couple steps back, bringing Jamie with her. The lynx tracked them with her eyes until Drake took another step forwards and blocked them from view completely.

Isolde understood what Drake was doing—he wanted the animal to focus on him and forget about her and Jamie. A part of her even recognized that it was the right thing to do. But Drake didn't have any weapons that could match the lynx's formidable teeth—teeth made for ripping and tearing. He could get badly hurt.

Still, she kept walking, because she'd promised him she would, and because they had to protect Jamie. She kept her arms tight around the boy, holding his body in front of hers—wondering if she'd hear the attack when it came.

Suddenly, there was a loud shuffling noise. Isolde turned to see Drake jumping backwards as the lynx raced across the path in front of him, disappearing on the other side.

"Fuck," Drake said loudly. "Sorry, Jamie."

"Is she gone?" Isolde asked.

Drake nodded. He leaned forwards, his hands on his knees, panting as if he'd run a long distance. Isolde understood the physiology of the body's response to stress, so she wasn't surprised at his reaction.

Jamie clasped her hand. Isolde looked down to comfort the boy, but he looked up at her, eyes shining. "Wow, wait till I tell my friends on Monday. Wait till I tell my dad, tonight."

Drake laughed. His gaze was still on the direction the lynx had left in. "Yeah, little guy, can't wait till your dad hears about this."

"How about we get back to the —?" Isolde said. Her heart was playing a staccato beat inside her chest. She wanted to get in the car and lock the doors behind them.

Drake nodded. "We're the second group to bump into this cat in the last week. I'll need to call animal protection services."

She and Drake fell into step together, keeping Jamie directly in front of them.

"What would you have done if she'd attacked?" Isolde asked.

Drake flexed his arm muscles. "I could have held my own."

"Yeah, you'd have made a great appetizer."

He shrugged, his expression going serious for a moment. "Maybe. Glad it didn't come to that. She was a beautiful animal."

By the time they arrived at Jamie's grandfather's place, Jamie was asleep in his car seat. Drake picked him up carefully, leaning the boy's cheek against his thick shoulder as he carried him into the house. Isolde watched from the car—her lower belly did a somersault as she watched the care Drake took not to wake the boy up.

A couple minutes later, Drake was back in the car.

"Are you okay, Isolde? You seem to be deep in thought."

She nodded quickly. "I'm fine."

He didn't start the car immediately.

"There's something I wanted to talk to you about."

"About the lynx?"

"No, nothing to do with the lynx," Drake said, running a hand across his square jaw.

"Okay?" she said. "I'm listening."

"I don't want to rush you, but I meant what I said last night." He took her hand in his much larger one. "Hear me out, please, before you say anything. I understand we're still getting to know each other again, and I don't want to rush you, but I'd like to do things right. I want us to tell the Colonel that we're together."

Isolde nodded slowly. It suddenly felt right, as if they'd been heading towards this the whole time, and this was inevitable.

"Okay," she finally said.

"Okay?"

"Okay. We'll take the risk."

"You make it sound like so much fun," he laughed. "Like a trip to the dentist."

"I'm sorry. I just—"

"Relax, Isolde. I'm just kidding. You make me happy," he said, looking almost surprised.

"You make me happy too."

16

Drake

A big storm was brewing—the kind that rarely came until November at the earliest. It hadn't broken yet, but the reports they got from the top showed the weather was already unsettled, with uneven visibility and strong winds.

At least Damien was back at work. He'd returned from his honeymoon looking tanned and more relaxed than Drake had seen him since—ever, actually. Damien's return had taken a load off Drake's shoulders. He thought back to the time he'd spent—if not wasted—in status meetings over the last weeks. He wasn't sure he was looking forward to his next promotion.

Drake had been hoping Damien's return would

mean some time off for him. He'd had been planning on taking Isolde to Lake Bourget for a surprise spa getaway weekend.

The upcoming storm had unfortunately put a hold on those plans—it was going to be all hands on deck until Monday morning.

Drake shook his head to clear the image of Isolde in a bathing suit at the Bourget thermal baths—he'd never been so angry at the sky before.

The team had spent most of the morning sharing the meteorological warning with everybody they met, attempting to drive people away from the mountains. Drake scratched his head as he thought of some of the more bizarre things people had said to him while he was trying to turn them away from the Goûter route.

"These trainers are really comfortable. I could climb Everest in them."

No. You couldn't.

"Don't worry about us, she loves walking."

It doesn't matter how much she loves it, she's four years old. Take her home. Come back in ten years.

"It's just a few clouds. We'll be back home by the time the storm breaks—if it breaks at all."

In a couple hours, visibility could be zero, the wind violent enough to rip you from the path.

It never failed to amaze Drake, how people thought they could just show up one day—no experience, no equipment, sometimes not even the right shoes—and attempt to climb Mont Blanc.

"I hate storms," Gael complained, rubbing his hands to keep them warm.

"That's because you can't climb in the rain," Hiro said. "Bailey doesn't like storms much either." He rubbed his dog's dark head of hair affectionately. Though Bailey was a Dutch Shepherd, and it would take weather a lot colder than this to make her uncomfortable, Hiro always carried a coat for her in his backpack. Just in case.

"That's because she's clever," Drake said. "Wish we could say the same about all the people we met this morning."

"At least some of them seemed to listen," Hiro said. "Each one of those is someone who won't get in trouble tonight."

Drake nodded. If they'd managed to stop just one person from going up the mountain in this weather, then the morning's activities could be considered a success.

"Any news from Damien, Kat and Jens?" Hiro asked.

Drake nodded, adjusting the zipper of his uniform jacket. It was starting to get cold.

"They just got back to headquarters. We should go back as well. There isn't much more we can do here."

Drake had the feeling it was going to be a long afternoon and night. Maybe he could spend a few minutes with Isolde before they had to head out again.

Isolde

Isolde rarely worked from home. Her job was all about meeting people, and that couldn't be done from her home office.

However, once a month she liked to schedule a "no patients Friday". She'd clear her schedule, stay home, and use that day to catch up on pending reports, review each one of her open cases, read up on sectoral trends she might be missing out on, and generally make sure she would be at her most productive over the following month.

She raised her eyes from her files and looked at the dark storm clouds looming. From the safety of her cozy home office, the sky was beautiful to look at, but she knew it would be a completely different story for anyone caught outside once the storm broke. She wriggled her feet inside the fluffy slippers she was wearing.

I couldn't have chosen a better day to work from home.

Even as she thought that, she couldn't help but think of Drake. Not that he minded a bit of bad weather—she'd spent enough time with him over the last weeks to know he went out running every day, regardless of the conditions outside. But still, she couldn't help but worry about him and the rest of the PGHM out there. The storm would make their job that much harder.

Her phone rang, and for a moment she wondered if it might be Drake.

"*Allô?*"

"It's Amélie."

A high-pitched whistling sound made Isolde move the cell phone further away from her ear.

"Amélie? I can't hear you very well, you're cutting out. Where are you?"

Amélie was silent so long, Isolde thought the connection must have broken. When she finally spoke, the young woman's voice was barely more than a whisper.

"I'm at the Bossons chairlift."

Isolde pulled the received back tightly against her ear.

"What are you doing up there, Amélie? You need to come back to town. There's a storm coming, you shouldn't be out—"

"You helped me understand that I don't want to live without Pierre."

Isolde could hardly hear Amélie's voice over the beating staccato of her heart. She stared at her phone as if she could pull the other woman through it.

"Amélie, where are you exactly? I need you to sit down and wait for me. I'm on my way."

"You'll come?" she asked. The other woman's voice sounded surprised, as if she hadn't expected it.

Isolde looked up at the looming clouds.

"I'll be there as soon as I can. Promise me you'll sit down and wait for me."

"I promise."

Isolde ran across her house. She was already wearing jeans, but she put on thick woolen socks and her winter hiking boots. She didn't take the time to do anything about her hair, which was piled on top of her head in a messy bun. Over the white long-sleeved top she was already wearing, Isolde put on a thin fleece. From a hook by the door she picked up her waterproof down jacket and ran outside to her car.

Please start, please start.

Thankfully, the engine came to life at the first try. The bottom station of the Bossons chairlift was only ten minutes away from her house, and she didn't imagine there would be a long line of people ready to get up there at this time of day, so that didn't concern her—what did worry her was the fact that the ride up was forty minutes long.

How long will Amélie wait for me?

What if she—

It didn't bear thinking about.

She needed to call Drake. Not just to tell him what was going on, but also because—if he and his team happened to be available and nearby—they might be able to reach Amélie Omont before she could.

Drake's phone rang once, twice, three times. With each ring, the chances he would pick up grew dimmer. Finally, the call went to his voice mail.

Shit.

She was too slow to leave a voice mail, so she had

to dial again. She waited impatiently for the voice mail to connect again, then spoke quickly before the machine disconnected her. She hated speaking to answering machines.

"Drake, it's Isolde. I'm on my way to the Bossons cable car. Amélie Omont is up there ... I'm worried she'll do something terrible. I'm going up to meet her now. If you happen to be in the area, please call me. Otherwise, I'll call you when I'm with her."

Isolde worried about the euphemism she'd chosen to use. *Something terrible.* Why couldn't she utter the action Amélie had actually threatened with.

She wondered if she should call the PGHM emergency number, or even the colonel. But the PGHM teams were probably all busy with the coming storm, and if Amélie was up waiting by the cable car, Isolde might be able to convince her to come down without having to take resources away from other rescues.

That was probably the best idea. Isolde owed it to Amélie—she owed it to Pierre—to find Amélie and bring her down safely if she could.

Drake

Drake leaned back against the SUV's headrest. Water dripped from his clothes and hair down onto the fabric of the seats. He was glad it was Damien driving rather than him. He was exhausted. Behind him sat

Gael and Hiro, while Bailey rested in a crate in the back of the SUV.

Behind him, Gael laughed.

"Man, that was wild, even for us."

Wild was one way to describe it. Drake wondered if he was getting old—he certainly wasn't as accepting of foolishness as he used to be.

"You do realize one of those men is the same one we warned away from the mountain just this morning, right? The one who told us he'd be back home and watching TV before the storm broke."

"Yeah, and we managed to extract him and his friend just in time. So they *will* get to watch TV tonight—even if they get to do it from a hospital room," Hiro said laconically.

"That was too close," Drake said. "Had they called us just a few minutes later, there's no way Kat would have been able to fly close enough. And they weren't equipped to survive the night at four thousand meters."

It'd been close. The wind and rain currently pummeling the SUV were nothing compared to what the storm was like higher up the mountain, where Kat had been flying. Had she been unable to approach, they would have had to launch a trekking rescue expedition to the Dome de Goûter, which would have meant walking half the night in bad visibility and fresh snow, with no guarantee of finding the climbers alive.

Damien's hands gripped the steering wheel.

"You're in a foul mood, Drake," Gael laughed. "Glad Jens is the one who rode with them in the helicopter, rather than you."

Drake grunted in response to the teasing.

He *was* in a foul mood. He hadn't been able to see Isolde earlier that day, since she'd been working from home.

Maybe he could stop by and—

His phone chimed a couple times as it picked up reception again. Drake fished it out of his sodden pocket, glad once again that he'd gotten a water-proof phone. He had two missed calls, both from Isolde. That was unusual—she rarely, if ever, called him during the day.

Maybe she's heard that I stopped by to see her at lunchtime.

He checked his voicemail service in case she'd left a message.

The sound of her voice thrilled him, but as he listened to her words, an unfamiliar weight settled on his chest. He wasn't ashamed to admit his first thoughts weren't for Amélie Omont—his concern was all for Isolde, who'd taken off for the mountains just before the storm broke.

Perhaps the chairlift was closed, perhaps she never made it —

That hope died as he listened to her second voice mail message. In this one, Isolde sounded slightly out of breath.

I'm at the top of the chairlift. Amélie isn't here. I'm going to go ask inside. I'll call you when I know more.

Drake gripped the phone tighter. He pressed the button to get to the next message. This time, Isolde's voice didn't make his heart beat faster. His heart was feeling too cold for that.

She's gone, Drake. I think she's trying to find the spot where Pierre jumped. I know you and the team are probably busy but ... if any of you are nearby, can you please call me back?

"Fuck."

"What's going on, Drake?" Damien asked quietly, not taking his eyes off the road.

Drake looked at the time. Five p.m. The message had been left almost two hours earlier.

"Isolde went up to the Bossons to find Amélie Omont, Pierre Omont's widow. Amélie was apparently threatening self-harm."

His friends muttered expletives under their breath. None of them had been close friends with Pierre Omont, but theirs was the kind of job where you bonded together. They all felt a responsibility to ensuring Pierre's wife didn't come to harm.

He called Isolde. The phone rang, and rang, and eventually went to voicemail. He didn't bother leaving a message.

"Fuck," Drake repeated.

"She went up in this storm?" Gael asked.

"Hell," Hiro said.

Drake nodded. In his mind, he was already

running through the different ways he could get to the Bossons Glacier. "Can you drop me off at the bottom of the chairlift, please? I need to get up."

"They're probably closed already, Drake, given the weather," Damien said.

"Fuck." Drake ran a hand through his hair. "Okay. Drop me off as close as you can to Le Mont. I'll walk."

In his mind, he was quickly running by the calculations. It'd take him a solid two hours to hike up to where he hoped Isolde was—and that was if he ran all the way up.

Hiro spoke up from the backseat—his phone was on his ear. "Kat just dropped Jens and the two patients off at the hospital. She was going to take the helicopter back to base but can meet us now and pick you up."

Thank God.

"Is that going to be safe for her?"

"Looks like the wind hasn't picked up there yet. But it's pouring. She's running low on fuel, though. You'll have to rappel down and make your own way back afterwards—or call in another chopper."

Drake nodded. Something gritty in both his eyes made them water. He rubbed at them with the back of his hand. When he looked back at his teammates, they were all staring at something else.

Drake knew this was a shitty time for him to disappear on his team.

"I'm sorry, Commandant," he told Damien. "I have to go do this."

Damien nodded. "You're not going alone, Drake. One of us will come with you."

Again, that inopportune bit of grit made his eyes water.

"No," he said in a quiet voice. "It's bad enough you're going to be short one man, plus Kat for a bit. I know it's going to be a busy evening, and I don't know when I'll be back. I'll find Isolde and Amélie and bring them back."

"You shouldn't be going alone," Damien insisted.

"We don't even know anything is wrong," he said, more to convince himself than the others. "Maybe it's just a connection issue, and Isolde and Amélie are on their way down already. I've got my radio. It'll be fine. I'll contact you if there's a problem."

Drake didn't need to say he'd find Isolde or die trying. His friends knew him well enough to know that was the case.

Less than ten minutes later, he was sitting in the helicopter with Kat.

"Thank you, Kat. This is ... I don't know how to thank you."

For a long instant, the pilot didn't answer. Her full focus was on the controls. Even if being inside a helicopter in this weather felt like being inside a tuna can set adrift in the ocean, Drake knew rain wouldn't affect Kat's ability to fly the machine. It did, however, impact visibility substantially, which meant she needed to be one hundred percent focused.

Once the weather cooled and the rain turned to

ice, that could also create a whole host of other problems for the machine.

"How about you shut up, and just get Isolde and Amélie back safe and sound?" the feisty pilot replied. "You're not the only one who likes Isolde, you know?"

Drake nodded. "I'll find her, Kat. No matter what. I'll try to bring them both home."

Kat went quiet. When she spoke, her voice was soft. "If Amélie is ... if she's done what she threatened she would do, Isolde is going to need you." It sounded to Drake like the pilot was talking about some personal experience in her life, but he didn't have time to delve into it as, just at that moment, the glacier came into sight.

The helicopter leaned to the side. Kat's hands were white on the controls as she struggled to hold the machine in place. The rain pelted the helicopter.

"There we are. You'll be okay rappelling down, right? It's not just the fuel situation. The fog's too dense for me to land."

"That's fine—much easier for me to figure out the landing than your ten-ton machine."

Fuck.
Talk about overconfident.

He'd almost killed himself rappelling down the helicopter into the fog. As it was, his weaker leg was shaking from the impact.

Most people assumed rappelling from a hovering helicopter was like rappelling down a mountain face. It was, in the same way as the Atlantic Ocean was similar to a garden pond. Rappelling down from a helicopter meant working on a moving target, as the ground moved up and down despite the pilot's best intentions. Add the storm into the equation, and even a pilot as skilled as Kat couldn't keep the helicopter still in the air for long.

As soon as he stepped out of the craft, he'd gone completely deaf—the only sound, that of his line zipping through the carabiners. He'd let out the rope fast, knowing every second he kept Kat up there was risking her life.

He didn't apply the brakes until he was twenty feet from the ground—but in the fog he'd miscalculated and hit a tree before falling to the ground like a lump. He was lucky he hadn't broken anything.

Man up. Isolde needs you.

He unclipped himself from the rope quickly and spoke into the short wave radio.

"Off the line. Thanks, Kat."

"I'm off to refuel, call me if you need me, Drake. Good luck."

Drake pulled his jacket tighter across his hips and neck. It was already going to be miserable enough out here without getting wetter than he needed to. He brought out his phone and dialed Isolde's number. The phone rang and rang. Drake disconnected it before it went to voice mail and put the sodden phone back in his inside pocket, close to his body, to protect the battery.

It was only five thirty p.m. but visibility was so low, it already felt like night was closing in. Drake pulled out his head lamp and put it over his forehead, then placed the hood back over his head. He turned the light on. Hiking alone was dangerous enough in the best of cases. Hiking alone in the middle of a storm without a head light was beyond foolish.

He turned to look at the top of the chairlift. He'd already spoken to the manager below while waiting for Kat to pick him up. He'd closed down at four p.m., when it became clear the storm would not pass them by. Chairlifts and heavy winds didn't mix, so the man's caution was understood.

The man remembered Isolde, since she'd been asking about another young woman—he hadn't been able to help her, though, as nobody remembered seeing the young woman. Then he'd turned to do something else, and by the time he'd looked back, Isolde was gone.

What happened, Isolde? Where did you go?

He looked down at his phone. Cell reception was strong here. It was possible she'd received another call from Amélie. Maybe the woman had taken the chairlift down and they were both at home right now.

But if so, why isn't she picking up the phone?

Damien had sent someone to check both Isolde and Amélie's home—but, until he got news back from that, Drake had to work on the assumption that Isolde was somewhere up in the mountains.

I'm going to find you, Isolde.

As far as he could see—which admittedly wasn't very far—everything was still. Suddenly, lighting splintered the air, a white-hot flash against the dark fog. It spurred Drake into motion. He wasn't going to find Isolde by standing out here in the storm.

17

Isolde

When she finally made her way to the top of the chairlift, Amélie Omont was nowhere to be found. After checking with the chairlift attendant, who did not remember seeing Amélie, Isolde followed the horde of visitors making their way to the nearby *chalet* for a warm drink.

Isolde was cautiously hopeful that Amélie would be there as well—the day had turned very cold, after all—but that hope died with a quick look inside the chalet.

No Amélie.

Until now Isolde had kept her fear and worry at bay by the promise she'd extracted from Amélie, that she'd wait up here by the chairlift. Now, though, those feelings swam to the front of her mind.

She wasted precious minutes talking to the *chalet* manager, who confided in her that he never looked at his guests, only at the food he served. He wouldn't know if Amélie had been there or not.

What matters is that she's not here now.

Where are you Amélie?

A fine drizzle covered her as she stood outside the building.

Great, just what I needed.

The line of visitors was moving in the other direction now. It seemed people had decided there was no point in being here in this drizzle—not when the descending fog wouldn't let them enjoy the view.

Isolde had never felt this alone in her life. She picked up her phone, praying she'd have a message from Drake. He would know what to do.

No message.

They were probably busy.

Isolde called again and left another message, letting him know Amélie wasn't there, and asking him to call her when he could.

Isolde squared her shoulders and brought out her thankfully plastic-coated map of the area. She hadn't come out here just to take the lift back down.

She needed to find Amélie.

Isolde ran her finger along the path that went from the *chalet* to the spot where Pierre had met his death. It was higher elevation, which meant the storm would most likely be worse up there.

How far ahead is she?

Only one way to find out.

Isolde tightened the pack around her shoulders. She wasn't an experienced hiker by any means, but in the years since she'd arrived in Chamonix she'd learned a few things. One of them was that a loose backpack would feel twice as heavy as a well-placed one, and cause much discomfort by the end of the hike.

As she walked, Isolde kept looking at her feet —the last thing she wanted was to trip on a rock and end up twisting her ankle.

She shouted Amélie's name until her throat felt raw. And, every so often but with increasing frequency the further she got from the *chalet*, she stopped to look at her map. Everything looked different in the descending fog, and she couldn't afford to take a wrong turn.

She wished Drake were here. Or Gael, who was a professional tracker—or, even better, Bailey. Even in this rain, they'd be able to track Amélie down with relative ease, whereas she might be walking right by Amélie and not see her if the woman didn't speak up.

It was at that point that Isolde realized she was in way over her head. She would call Drake again and, if he didn't pick up, she'd call the PGHM hotline. Her fingers were colder than she's realized—it took her a couple tries just to get the phone out of her pocket, only to discover she was in a dead zone.

Shit.

She was going to need to backtrack until she reached an area with phone coverage.

Tears filled her eyes, and she wiped them away angrily. She'd come all this way because she wanted to help Amélie, but she'd overestimated her capabilities out here. She needed help.

Sighing, Isolde turned to head back down, conscious of the edge to her left side—there was the valley beneath her feet, the ground a few hundred feet below.

Suddenly, Isolde heard a sound off behind the path. Her heart seized, thinking of the lynx she, Drake and Jamie had seen just a few weeks earlier.

Don't be ridiculous, Isolde.

They found that lynx.

But what if there's another one?

"Amélie?" Isolde whispered.

The bushes rustled. Isolde sighed in relief when she saw Amélie's body appear from behind the greenery.

"Amélie, thank God. I've been looking everywhere for you."

"You found me," Amélie said. She was wrapped up in a thick winter jacket, but still shivering in the cold.

"Listen, we need to make our way back to the *chalet*," Isolde said. "We'll be safe there. The storm's going to get a lot worse before it gets better."

"It is."

Something about Amélie's tone sent a shiver up Isolde's spine.

"Amélie? How long have you been out here?" Hypothermia was a serious concern if she'd been standing out here for a long time.

Amélie wasn't looking at her. Instead, she looked off towards the valley below. Isolde didn't like the glacial expression on her face.

"Did you come alone?" Amélie asked, looking all around them.

"Yes. I was worried, Amélie, we need to—"

"Good."

Good?

The shiver intensified.

"Amélie, come on, we need to get out of here."

Amélie didn't react to her words. Instead, she began speaking in a strange monotone.

"What I told you on the phone was true, you know. I've realized I can't go on without Pierre."

"It'll get easier, Amélie, it'll—"

Amélie raised her hand imperiously, raising her voice. "No. What I mean is, I don't *want* to go on without Pierre." Her eyes narrowed. "But I don't think Pierre and I should be the only ones to pay. Not when *you* were the one who let him die."

"What?"

"He trusted you. The last time he went to see you,

he was so relaxed afterwards. Somehow, I think you put the idea in his mind."

The jab hit deep. Isolde had often wondered exactly the same thing—if Pierre could have misinterpreted anything she said. The fog made it hard to think—it surrounded their bodies but also seemed to be clouding her mind.

Had Pierre given any warning that day that she'd ignored?

Isolde steeled herself against the familiar guilt. She couldn't change what had happened a year earlier—but she could still try to help Amélie.

"No. You have to listen to me, Amélie, I had no idea. I would never—"

"I knew you'd try to talk your way out of this." The young woman's eyebrows almost joined together in the middle of her forehead, her face a mask of hatred. "It's what you do, right? You've convinced everyone that it wasn't your fault."

"As much as I regret Pierre's death, it *wasn't* my fault, Amélie," Isolde said softly. "Come on, let's head back down and talk about this."

Amélie went on as if Isolde hadn't spoken.

"I'll let you in on a secret. When Pierre died, I was pregnant. I hadn't told him yet. It was my secret. I was almost three months along, but he was so sad about that stupid job, it never seemed like the right moment to tell him. So I waited."

"Oh no, Amélie," Isolde said. "I'm so sorry." Her hand reached out towards the woman, even though there were still a few bodies of air between them. "What happened to the baby?"

"*It happens sometimes,* the doctors said. But I think the baby just wanted to go with Pierre. And now, it's time for me to join them both."

Isolde's heart thundered. She wondered if she was the only one who could hear it.

"It's not the answer, Amélie. I know it hurts now, but—"

"Shut up, just shut up," Amélie said. She pressed her hand against her temple, hard. "You weren't there when Pierre needed you, and he took his own life. Now you're going to jump too."

"*What?* Have you lost your mind, Amélie?"

In response, Amélie dug into her backpack and came up with a gun. She brought the barrel up, so it pointed straight at Isolde. Fury burned in the widow's eyes.

"Is that Pierre's weapon?" Isolde asked, unnecessarily.

"Nobody ever asked me for it, so I kept it. As a souvenir—I never thought I'd use it. But it's fitting, isn't it? I've been practicing in the forest. If you don't jump, I'll have to shoot you."

Isolde was frozen in terror. She dug her nails into her palms and took a deep breath.

Isolde imbued her shaking voice with as much strength as she could. "I'm not going to jump, Amelie."

Amélie tightened her finger on the trigger.

Oh, God.

"She's not going to jump."

Isolde turned her head at the low, rough voice. Through the fog, she couldn't see the anybody, but she didn't need to see him to know Drake was there.

"She's got a gun, Drake!" Isolde shouted as Amélie pointed the weapon towards the voice. She should have been relieved to find the weapon no longer pointed in her direction, but the thought of Drake getting shot was more than she could bear.

Drake walked through the fog towards them. He looked big and solid. Isolde wanted to run to him and wrap herself against him—but knew that would probably only get them both killed.

He walked towards them slowly, his hands open by his sides, trying to make himself look as unthreatening as possible. He was breathing hard, as if he'd been running for a long time.

Isolde sneaked a look at Amélie. Fury burned in the woman's eyes.

"You told me you came alone. You *lied* to me," she spat out. It was testament to her delusion that she actually considered herself the injured party in all this.

Drake had stopped his approach, forcing Amélie to shift the gun between Isolde and him. His hair was dripping wet, making it look almost black.

"I came on my own," Drake said, speaking in a hushed tone. "I'm going to bring you both home."

"You can go back down the way you came. I have

nothing against you. This is between the doctor and me."

Drake's eyebrow went up, and Isolde knew the next words that came out of his mouth were not going to please Amélie.

"Yes, get out of here, Drake," Isolde said. She couldn't bear to see him get hurt. She tried to signal Drake with her eyes, hoping he'd understand what she was trying to tell him.

Get out of here and get help.

In response, Drake snorted.

He actually snorted.

Amélie's jaw hung open for a second. Instants later, her expression was transformed by fury.

"You're laughing at me?" she whispered.

"I'm not laughing at you, Amélie. I'm laughing at your suggestion that I might turn around and leave Isolde here—"

"Drake ..." Isolde said carefully, dreading the next words out of his mouth, but Drake forged on.

"—with someone who is so clearly unbalanced."

Amélie snarled.

"Drake!" Isolde said.

"Not the word you would have chosen, Doc?" he asked, smiling.

She understood what he was trying to do—he was trying to turn Amélie's anger onto himself. But to what purpose?

Is he standing closer to Amélie than he used to be?

"You shouldn't be here," Amélie hissed. "It should

just be the two of us. Dr. Durant and I are going to jump," Amélie insisted stonily, her voice devoid of emotions.

"Over my dead body," Drake snarled back.

"No! Drake!" Isolde screamed.

Amélie kept the gun on Drake. "Walk closer to the edge, Isolde. *Now*. Or I'll shoot him instead."

Isolde took a couple small steps forward. She was now much closer to the edge than she'd ever wanted to be. She'd never suffered from a fear of heights, but then again she'd never been—

"I'll give you one last chance," Amélie said, in a coaxing voice. "If you jump, I'll let him l—"

She never got the chance to finish the sentence. Drake lunged, moving faster than she'd ever seen a person move before, tackling Amélie to the ground. The gun clattered uselessly behind her. Isolde shuffled back from the edge, her heart in her mouth.

Drake was twice Amélie's body weight, but it was clear he was trying not to hurt the woman. He reached out with his hand to push the gun further away from them, and that's when Amélie sneaked out from underneath him. She was on her feet and running for the edge in an instant, shouting Pierre's name.

Isolde shouted as the woman leaped to her death before them—only to be caught by Drake, who'd hurled himself in her direction and managed to hold on to Amélie's wrist at the very last instant. He was on his stomach, his upper body hanging off the ledge, his hold on Amélie's wrist the only thing stopping her from falling to her death.

Amélie dangled in Drake's grasp, cursing a blue streak.

"Stop ... stop moving," he said, speaking through clenched teeth.

Isolde kneeled beside him.

"Get back, Isolde, away from the edge," he grunted. Then, in a louder voice, speaking to Amélie. "I won't let you fall, Amélie, I promise."

Amélie's right hand came up. For a moment, Isolde thought she was going to grab on to Drake's arm to help him—then she saw the glinting metal in her hand.

The knife sliced deep into Drake's right arm. Drake roared in pain. His left hand swiped at the hand holding the knife, which fell into the abyss. But he never let go of Amélie's wrist.

"Let me go, you bastard," Amélie screamed.

Red blood dripped down Drake's arm. Soon, it would reach his hand, where he was holding on to Amélie.

She's going to slip.

Drake seemed to remember he had a free arm, the one he'd used to swipe away at the knife. He wrapped his left hand around Amélie's arm, so he was now holding on to her arm with both hands.

"I'm not ... going to let you drop." With a grunt, Drake started lifting.

It took Isolde a moment to realize that Amélie

wasn't screaming obscenities at them anymore—at some point over the last seconds, she'd passed out.

Finally, Amélie's shoulders were level with the top of the cliff. Drake didn't stop pulling. Isolde reached out to grab on to Amélie's armpits and pulled, taking Amélie's weight onto herself.

Drake was on his feet in a matter of seconds, grabbing Amélie off of Isolde. He lay the woman down flat on the floor and placed two fingers on her neck.

Isolde held her breath.

"She's okay—just passed out," Drake said. He turned Amélie's body on to her side and pulled out a pair of zip ties.

"Is that necessary?"

Drake didn't raise his eyes to look at her until he'd finished tying Amélie's wrists together in front of her body. "Are you *kidding* me?" he replied, his tone incredulous.

Fair enough.

Maybe not the right question to ask.

"Uh, Drake ... you're bleeding everywhere," Isolde said. Blood pumped out steadily from the cut in his arm. She noticed for the first time that his face looked almost gray.

How much blood is he losing?

"Yeah," he said. He pulled up his sleeve to look at the wound. "Looks worse than it is ... I think."

Unconvinced, Isolde reached into her backpack and grabbed a small towel she always carried with her. It was still mostly dry.

"Here, put pressure on it," she said. "We need to stop the bleeding."

He winced but didn't make a sound.

"Thanks."

Overhead, lighting flashed, followed by thunder. The storm was right on top of them.

"What are we going to do now, Drake?"

He was already on his radio. "Kat, I found them. They are both fine but it was a close call."

"Thank God, Drake. Where are you now? The storm is getting worse. The colonel has grounded all birds until tomorrow at oh six hundred."

Isolde's stomach sank.

How are we going to get Amélie off this mountain?

Drake's voice remained calm. "I understand."

There was a pause, then Kat's voice said quietly. "But if you need me—"

Drake didn't hesitate. "No. We'll be okay. I'll share the coordinates with you so you can pick us up tomorrow morning."

"We'll be here if you need anything."

Isolde bit her lip to keep from crying out loud. Her fear had kept the cold and exhaustion at bay for a little while, but in the aftermath of the crisis her body was starting to crash, and the thought of spending the night out here in the storm filled her with terror. The white towel she'd given him was already soaked red.

She hoped Drake had a plan.

"Don't worry," he said, putting the radio back in

his pocket. "It's going to be okay, Isolde. I'm trained to handle this."

As if in response to his reassuring words, the skies opened up. The constant drizzle of the last hour became a downpour.

"Fuck," he said. "We can't stay here. This volume of water can easily cause a landslide up here."

He was right. Small rivers of mud, carrying larger rocks and other debris, were already making their way down the slope. If it rained hard enough, soon it would be larger rocks, and even trees.

Isolde shivered.

Drake took her hand in hers. "There's a cave near here where we can stay until the morning."

"A cave? Won't other animals have had the same idea?"

"I've never seen any animals there before. But I'll check before we go in, I promise."

"What about Amélie?"

Drake crouched in front of Amélie's unconscious body and pulled on her bound arms gently, lifting her onto his shoulders in a fireman's carry. He straightened easily to his feet, balancing Amélie on his shoulders.

"How far is this cave?" she asked carefully.

18

Isolde

He'd lied to her—by implication, at least. They'd been walking for what seemed like hours, and there was still no sign of the cave.

Drake shifted the unconscious woman on his shoulders. Though he didn't make a sound, his jaw tensed. Isolde flinched in sympathy. He'd all but admitted he'd raced up the mountain to find her, and his arm must be hurting.

The small towel she'd wrapped around it was drenched in blood. Isolde wasn't that kind of doctor, but she knew enough to know they'd need to stop and take care of it sometime soon.

A gust of wind caught her and almost threw her onto the ground. Drake reached out a steadying arm.

"You okay?" he asked gruffly. Then his voice softened a little. "We're almost there."

Isolde nodded but didn't waste any energy replying. As much as she liked to understand and control everything in her environment, in this case she knew she simply had to trust him.

Soon she was cold enough she couldn't feel her toes anymore, but she kept going. Stopping would only expose them further, and it wasn't like he could carry her out of here, anyway, not without letting go of Amélie.

Isolde's heart clenched when she thought of how close they'd come to losing Amélie.

"Is she okay?" she asked.

"Still breathing," he said. His eyebrow lifted. "You really care about her, don't you?"

"Of course I do. She needs help, Drake."

"She tried to kill you."

"She's hurting. She needs help."

He looked at her for the longest time. "You're a better person than I am," he said, finally.

"Not really. You're the one carrying her."

"That's different." They walked on in silence until, finally, he pointed up the mountain. "There it is!" he said.

Even though Isolde couldn't see three feet beyond her, his enthusiasm was contagious. She pushed herself that extra distance until she finally saw what he was talking about. It looked more like a hole in the wall than a cave, but at least inside they'd be protected from the rain.

Drake dropped the unconscious woman gently on the ground. "Stay with her," he asked. He began a thorough inspection of the area outside the cave, looking for any sign that an animal had chosen to set residence there, she assumed.

After a minute, he walked inside the cave. His large body disappeared from view almost immediately—the cave must be bigger than it'd looked from the outside. Isolde counted the seconds.

One Mississippi. Two Mississippi. Three Mississippi.
Where the hell did he go?

She thought of the lynx, and all the other animals that could have been hiding inside the cave, just waiting for Drake to step in. She wondered if she should leave Amélie and go inside to look for him, but what if—

Finally, he came back outside. He was no longer wearing his backpack. Isolde swayed in relief and exhaustion, almost going down to her knees. He ran to her side and placed a steadying hand on her waist.

"I'm okay, it's just—"

"I know. I'm sorry I'm asking so much of you. We'll be safe inside—and dry."

"Dry? Don't tempt me with such words, Drake," aiming for humor. She didn't miss the dark, smoldering look in his eyes.

"I'll be sure to keep that in mind, now that I know *dry* turns you on," he whispered in her ear.

He wrapped his left arm tighter around her. "Come on, let's get you inside."

"What about Amélie?"

"I'll come back for her in a minute. I want you out of the storm, Isolde."

"Take her in, please. I can walk."

I couldn't bear it if anything happens to her.

She didn't say that last bit out loud.

Drake looked like he was about to argue with her, but eventually he nodded. In a swift, efficient move, he had Amélie over his left shoulder.

Isolde noticed he was using his right arm less and less. Blood still dripped down his hand.

How much blood has he lost?

"Grab on to my belt, Isolde."

Twice Isolde started to slide, and it was only her hold on Drake's belt bucket that kept her from rolling all the way to the bottom again. Finally, together, they made it up to the cave's mouth. It was much bigger than it'd looked from outside. Drake could stand up comfortably inside, which meant she'd have no trouble.

And it was *dry*. Isolde shivered.

She watched him drop Amélie on top of a small tarp he'd prepared ahead of time. He put his fingers to her neck for what seemed to Isolde a long time.

"Her pulse is steady." He covered the unconscious woman with a space blanket, pulling it up to her neck.

"You're going to leave her hands tied?"

"You bet I am," he replied. "I won't get any rest if I'm worried she's going to try to kill you again, Isolde."

Amélie's earlier erratic behavior bothered her. "It just didn't seem like her, Drake. We need to speak with her doctor and—"

"Her hands stay tied, Isolde."

Isolde nodded.

"Shit. I'm bleeding everywhere," he muttered. "I'm going to need your help, Doc," he said.

"You know I'm not that kind of doctor, right?" Her expression softened as she took note of his clenched jaw. "Does it hurt a lot?"

He shook his head. "Pain, I can handle. But it should have stopped bleeding already."

Isolde walked closer to him.

"God, you're beautiful," he said.

She touched her dripping wet hair. Her ponytail had come undone. She was so tired she hadn't even noticed. "Yeah, dripping hair is the new fashion statement. How can I help, Drake? Please tell me you don't want me to stitch it up."

He laughed softly. "Don't worry. I've got some tape."

"Tape?" she said, worried. "Is that even safe?"

"We just need something to close the wound for now. Whatever we do, it's only temporary. The doctors at the hospital will open up the wound again when I get there, to clean it out."

"That sounds ... painful."

He took off his jacket and placed it on the ground

to dry. From a side pocket of his backpack, he brought out a small pouch.

"First aid kit," he said. "Never leave home without it."

"I'll have to remember that."

Isolde realized she'd come out here woefully unprepared, expecting to simply meet Amélie at the top of the chairlift and—

"Hey, it's okay, relax, Isolde. I can do this myself."

"No. I'll help. I'm sorry, I was just ... thinking."

He nodded, his eyes focused on her. She wondered how she'd ever thought Drake's eyes cold.

He raised his sleeve to reveal a long, angry cut. It looked deep—Isolde could see the muscle layers exposed underneath.

"This is good."

"Is it?" she asked, swallowing hard.

"It's almost stopped bleeding." He picked up something from his pack and started spreading it liberally on the wound. His lips formed a tight, white line.

"Is that going to help?"

"Just some antibacterial ointment."

Next, Drake dried the area with a clean gauze. He handed her the duct tape.

"Okay, this is what we're going to do. I'll bring the edges of the cut together. You're going to tear off several strips of duct tape and place them perpendicular to the wound, okay? Like that, as tight as you can."

She kneeled beside him and started working. Even though he didn't make a sound, she could see in the lines of his jaw that he was hurting.

"So you're one of those, huh," she said to distract him.

Drake arched an eyebrow. "One of those?"

"You know, people who think duct tape can fix any problem."

He laughed. "I guess I *am* one of those."

"I'm starting to understand. I'll get myself some duct tape when we're home," she promised.

"I've got lots of it at home. I'll share it with you." His eyes were full of promise.

She placed the last strip tightly on his arm. Drake flexed his arm, testing the tape. "This should work. Thanks, Isolde."

"Do you have any painkillers?" she asked uncertainly.

He was on her in a second, his eyes roaming her from head to toe.

"Are you hurt?"

She shook her head. "Not for me—for you."

He sagged in relief. "God, you scared me. I'm fine. I told you before, I can handle pain."

"But ..."

"Sit down, Isolde. Before you drop."

Drake guided her down onto his coat. "No," she complained. "You'll freeze."

"Relax. I'm going to start a small fire at the overhang."

"Is that safe?" she asked. She'd heard of people dying due to poor air circulation.

"Safe enough. The entrance is large, so air will still be able to circulate, but we'll be warmer inside."

Isolde watched as he set to the task. She was reminded once again how unprepared she was, both in terms of equipment and knowledge.

You came up here with little more than a water bottle.

What would you have done if Drake hadn't shown up?

She shivered. The only thing she knew for sure was, she wouldn't have jumped.

Minutes later the small round fire crackled. Just looking at the fire made her feel warmer.

Drake fired off a quick message to his teammates. "Good news. Damien remembers this cave. They'll be here to pick us up first thing tomorrow, as soon as the storm breaks."

"What do we do in the meantime?"

"We wait here. We try to stay as warm as possible."

"What about Amélie? I'm worried about her. She's been unconscious for a long time."

Drake shrugged. "Her pulse was steady enough. She had a shock to her system. Jens will come with Damien so he can assess the situation. In the meantime, all we can do is keep her warm and hydrated."

Isolde kneeled beside the young woman.

"She could have died, Drake."

"Excuse me if I'm not as sympathetic as you,

Isolde. She wanted to kill you." He flexed his muscles. "I'm not going to let her, or anybody else, hurt you."

Drake

Drake clenched his hands, which made pain flare up his arm. Amélie had really done a number on his arm—pretty amazing considering she'd had almost no leverage from her hanging position.

He watched the slim woman now. Unconscious, she looked completely harmless, but Drake wasn't going to forget the dead look in her eyes as she'd asked Isolde to jump.

The moment he'd left the chairlift, he'd started running. Something told him Isolde needed him. When he'd finally seen the two figures emerge through the fog, he'd breathed a sigh of relief, until he'd realized what was happening.

You're going to jump.

Amélie's words would stay with him for as long as he lived.

Isolde sat on his coat, her hands stretched out towards the fire. She looked fragile and vulnerable, and he wanted to reassure her—and himself.

"Are you okay?" he asked, kneeling beside her.

Isolde nodded, but her eyes were unfocused. "Amélie had a few sips of water, but it looks like she's sleeping now."

"Have *you* had any water, Isolde?"

She shook her head.

"It won't do Amélie any good if you don't take care of yourself. That's the first rule of search & rescue."

"Is it?" Isolde asked, incredulous. "Have you had any water yourself? Because it seems to me all you've done since this whole thing started is take care of us."

He could tell her he knew exactly how long he could go without water before being incapacitated, but he didn't think that would appease Isolde.

"It's time for both of us to have some water, then," he said. He pulled out his water bottle from the pack and tipped the water towards his mouth, though he only had a small sip. He then took her smaller hand in his and handed her the bottle.

For a moment, Isolde refused to take it. Drake waited patiently.

"What if we run out of water, Drake? How much water do we even have? I came so unprepared. I put on my hiking boots and waterproof and ran out the door after Amélie called me. I wouldn't even have my water bottle except it'd been in my backpack and I refilled it at the chairlift before I started walking. What was I *thinking*?"

Her last words were full of pain.

Drake carefully put the cap on the water bottle and set it on the ground beside them. "Come here, Isolde," he said, putting his arms around her. She stood stiffly inside his embrace for a moment, but he pressed on until she eventually relaxed. Her arms came around his middle. Her touch branded him.

"I didn't know how Amélie was feeling, I wouldn't have known how to keep her alive, and if you'd died—" she sobbed.

Drake took each of those in turn. "I didn't die, Isolde. I'm fine, and I'm here with you. We're going to do our best to keep Amélie safe, and to get her the help she so clearly needs. And you couldn't have known how she was feeling. First of all, because she isn't your patient, but also because you aren't a mind reader. I know you've heard this before, but this isn't on you."

He offered her the water bottle again. Isolde sniffled, looking up at him, but this time she drank. "You have answers for everything?"

"Come here, sweetheart."

Isolde's cheek felt warm against his chest.

"Thank you, Drake. For everything."

Drake lifted her chin gently until they were looking directly at each other. The light from the fire shone in her honey-colored eyes.

He rubbed the heel of his palm against his eyes. "Jesus, when I think of how close I came to losing you, Isolde. You know I would do anything for you, right?"

He leaned down to kiss her forehead, needing the contact with her more than he needed his next breath, but her face came up at the last second, so his lips fell on her mouth instead. Drake's desire ignited the moment his rough lips met Isolde's soft lips. Then her lips parted slightly and her pink tongue came out, tracing the shape of his lips.

His eyes closed in pleasure as they explored each other's mouths tenderly.

I love you.

The words were on the tip of his tongue, about to leave his mouth, when something suddenly moved to the side of them. Drake instinctively positioned himself between Isolde and the sound, until he realized it was just Amélie, thrashing around in the midst of a nightmare.

Isolde rushed to the woman's side and held her bound hands, whispering soothing words.

"She's cold, Drake."

Drake fished in his backpack and came up with a slim sleeping bag. He shook it out to fluff it up, then unzipped the two halves.

"Here," he said, wrapping one half of the sleeping bag around Amélie, right over the space blanket. "This should help trap warm air around her. Come on, Isolde, you need to get warm and rest as well."

"I'm okay," she said, but got up and followed him back to the other side of the cave. She sat on his coat, her back against the wall, leaving space for him on the other side.

Drake sat down next to her, dropping his pack beside him. He wrapped the sleeping bag tight around both of them.

"How are you feeling, Isolde?"

She considered for a moment.

"Hungry," she said.

He laughed out loud. "Here, have this," he said, pulling a power bar out of his pocket. He knew she wouldn't eat the whole thing, so he broke it in half and started chewing on his half while offering the other piece to her.

She moaned appreciatively when the flavor hit her mouth—the sound going straight to his cock. Drake was glad now for the sleeping bag that covered his lap.

"You really are just like Mary Poppins," she said, speaking around a mouthful. Then her expression got serious again. "Are we safe here, Drake?"

"You can rest, Isolde. I won't let anything hurt you."

"We can take turns keeping watch. I don't want you to stay up all night."

"I'm okay, I need little sleep. Rest, please, Isolde. You'll need your energy tomorrow morning."

He didn't know when he'd be able to close his eyes again and not see Amélie waving her gun at Isolde—but that day wouldn't be tonight.

He felt the moment her body relaxed against his. For hours he stayed still, unwilling to risk waking her up.

Outside, the storm raged—but inside the cave, Drake's body was attuned to every small change in Isolde's breathing pattern. A couple times she moaned and shuddered. Each time that happened,

Drake grabbed her hands gently and whispered in her ear, which seemed to help quieten her down.

His flashlight was dying, its small light now yellow and faint, but it would last them the night. Drake kept it on because he wanted—no, he needed—to see Isolde. To know that she was really okay. He'd been given a second chance with her, and he wasn't going to mess it up.

19

Isolde

Isolde hobbled out of the shower, feeling more human than she had going in, even though her body was bruised and sore.

She was fine, of course—at Drake's insistence, she'd been checked out by Jens in the helicopter, then again by a doctor at the hospital.

The last time she'd seen Drake had been at the hospital. It'd been his turn to get his arm *checked out*, which she understood was code for something painful—Isolde had wanted to stay with him, but one of the hospital psychiatrists had chosen that exact moment to ask her questions about Amélie.

She'd been grilled for two hours, by the psychiatrist and by a policewoman, until she'd asked them if she could please go home, shower, and continue the conversation later on. At that point, they'd run out of questions.

Isolde dried herself briskly. Although her body probably needed the pampering now more than ever, she was in too much of a rush to bother with body moisturizer or with blow drying her hair. Instead, she left her hair loose, and used a dark blue velvet headband to keep it out of her eyes. She dressed quickly in black pants and a long-sleeved top that covered some of her bruises and scrapes, grabbed her large handbag, and went outside.

Puddles on the ground all the way to the car showed her just how bad the storm had been, even down here—up there in the mountains, she wasn't sure she would have survived the night, even if she had been able to escape Amélie.

Recognizing the gritty feeling behind her eyes as exhaustion, Isolde drove carefully.

It was lunchtime on a Saturday, and she made it all the way up the elevator and into her office without seeing anybody. She sat down gratefully and opened her laptop.

Less than two minutes later, Colonel Pelegrin himself knocked on her door.

The colonel was the kind of man who rarely raised his voice—he didn't need to.

"Dr. Durant," he said, "What *are* you doing here?"

"I'm working, Colonel," she said. "I often work on Saturday mornings." She didn't want to be coddled.

"Just because I was stupid enough to almost get killed out there, doesn't mean—"

"Let me stop you right there. What you did was not stupid. It was foolhardy—"

"I called the PGHM," she reminded him.

"You called one man. When he didn't answer, you should have called the PGHM hotline and had a team come with you to find *Madame* Omont." He raised his hand, ending the discussion. "But I didn't come here to argue with you. I'm here to ask why you're not taking the day off and resting, the way the doctors asked you to."

Isolde blushed.

"You're part of my team, Isolde. We need you back in top form. So take some time off."

Isolde felt tears pooling in the back of her eyes and blinked them away. She'd rather die than cry in front of her boss, a man who'd probably never shed a tear in his life.

"There's something I need to jot down, Colonel. An idea I came up with last night ..."

He seemed curious—and also aware that she wasn't going to let it go.

"Tell me about this idea," he said, sitting down in one of the chairs in front of her.

"Amélie Omont was ... " Isolde swallowed. Her tongue felt thick in her mouth. "I'm sorry."

"Take your time, Isolde. We're in no rush."

Isolde nodded. The plan had come to her at night, just before she'd fallen asleep on Drake's shoulder.

"We have an awareness and prevention program in place for all *gendarmes*."

The colonel nodded, encouraging her to continue.

"Exceptionally, we work with families as well—we've helped coordinate couples' counseling, several times, for gendarmes who were going through a rough patch in their marriage, for example. But we don't have a formal program in place for families—and we *should*, Colonel. When you see what Pierre Omont's death did to Amélie ... and all she got from us were flowers and a card after his death. She's been alone this whole year, trying to cope with her grief—"

"She tried to kill you, Isolde. Jacobs told me what happened."

Isolde straightened her spine. "I know that. I'm not trying to hide or excuse what she did. But I know she didn't want to hurt *me* personally—she wanted to get back at *us*, for failing Pierre and for failing her."

The colonel nodded. "What do you have in mind?"

"I think we need a formal program directly for and with families—we need to make sure we identify high-stress situations so they don't escalate to the point that ... this one did. We need to address the needs of wives, husbands, partners and children." She stopped to take a deep breath. "You probably think it's crazy." she said.

The colonel took his time answering. "It's not

crazy. It's a great idea. Put the plan together and think of the resources you need. We'll make it happen."

"Really?" she asked. "Just like that? I thought ..."

"What did you think, Isolde?"

She had the good sense to shut up. "Nothing, Colonel. Thank you, Colonel. You'll have the plan in place tomorrow."

"Not tomorrow. On Tuesday. This weekend, I want you to go home and get some sleep."

"But I just got here."

"Then get yourself back home, Dr. Durant. Or get Jacobs to drive you back. I need you back in top shape on Monday."

The colonel left without another word. Isolde spent twenty minutes jotting some urgent reminders to herself—interventions she knew the program needed to include, things to look out for, things she couldn't afford to forget.

When she looked up again, Drake was standing outside her office. He looked strong and ready to take on the world. The duct tape was gone—his forearm was covered in a thick, gauzy bandage instead.

"Shouldn't you be resting?" he asked gruffly.

"Shouldn't *you*?" she retorted.

He nodded sheepishly. "Yes," he said. "I'm exhausted, and my arm is killing me."

"You're not just saying that to get me to go home with you? Did the colonel tell you I was here?"

"The colonel didn't need to tell me. Everybody's talking about the fact that you're here today, after what happened. That's some insane dedication to the job, Isolde."

Now it was her turn to blush.

"Come on. I haven't had anything to eat since this morning at the hospital, and I'll bet you haven't either."

At the mention of food, her stomach rumbled. She looked down at her phone. It was three p.m.

"Come with me, I have food at home. We're taking the afternoon off."

20

Drake

Over the next few weeks, Isolde worked tirelessly to bring the new program to life.

Word of what she was trying to do—and support for the initiative—spread quickly around the *gendarmerie*. Nobody wanted to become Pierre Omont, but what really drove fear into the hearts of *gendarmes* was the thought of what had happened to Amélie after Pierre's death.

Drake was proud of the way Isolde had made something positive of an awful situation.

Because waiting outside her house was pointless now that she was working so late, he'd taken to looking for her in the office on his way home, on the days when he had a day shift, to bring her home with him.

He knocked gently on her open office door. Isolde took off her reading glasses, blinking a couple times to focus her eyes. A smile lit her face as she recognized him. Drake's cock hardened in response but he pointedly ignored it.

"You're smiling big today," he said.

"It's been a good day. The colonel kept up his side of the bargain. He's given me the resources I asked for, so François and I have started looking for a psychologist to take over the program."

"That's great. You can tell me all about it on the way home."

"Home?" Isolde sounded surprised. "What time is it?"

"Almost nine p.m."

"Wow, the day really flew by."

"Come on. That way I won't have to worry about you driving that tin can you call a car."

She laughed. "Is that the only reason you came to see me?"

"Not the only reason. I'm also hoping you'll let me take your clothes off tonight."

At his words, Isolde's pupils got wider. She worried her lower lip gently with her teeth. Drake barely kept himself from groaning.

The woman has no idea what she does to me.

At the parking garage, they bumped into his friend Hugo.

"How are you, man?" Drake said, clapping him on the back. "We'll meet at the gym on Tuesday morning?"

His friend smiled widely. "Looking forward to kicking your ass, Drake, as usual." He turned towards Isolde and was silent for an instant, as if debating whether to say something. "Pretty impressive work you're doing, Dr. Durant. I have a wife and two little boys ... so I wanted to say thank you."

Isolde blushed the prettiest color. "Any ideas you or your colleagues have, I would love to hear them, Hugo. I will do everything in my power to make sure we do this right."

After a couple minutes of chit-chat, Hugo left. Drake pressed the fob and unlocked the doors to his car.

"You've become a bit of a rock star, Isolde," he laughed.

Isolde went very serious. "That's not what I—"

"Hey. I'm kidding. I know that. Everybody knows that."

"Good. Good. It's not my program, you know. It needs to be everyone's program."

"And it will be. Relax, Isolde. You're doing all the right things."

She nodded, still looking worried. "Drake, can I ask you something?"

"Anything."

"I spoke with the psychiatrist at the hospital this morning."

"The one treating Amélie?"

Isolde nodded. "Amélie's doing much better now. Her mother has come down from Paris to be with her, and she's finally getting the professional help she needs. Her doctor thinks that having a session together with us would be good for her file, when it comes time for the authorities to review it."

Drake forced himself to loosen his hold on the steering wheel. "Is that a good idea?" he asked, careful to keep his voice steady.

"I know she hurt you," Isolde continued, pointing at his arm, "and that it might not be easy for you to—"

"You really think that's what bothers me?" he asked. He felt his pulse skyrocket.

"You're human, Drake. You were attacked—"

Drake didn't answer until he'd parked outside his apartment building. He unclipped his seatbelt and turned towards her. He grabbed her small hand lightly in his. "Every time I close my eyes, Isolde, I see her pointing that gun at you and asking you to jump. I need to know you're thinking of yourself, not just of Amélie's well-being."

Her eyes filled with tears. "Oh, Drake ..."

His hands went around her. "The thought that I could have lost you ... it tears me apart."

"You didn't lose me, Drake. You're not going to lose me. But Amélie—"

"If you want me there, I'll be there."

Her eyebrows arched up in surprise. "You will?"

"Of course I will. I'm not letting you do this alone."

21

Isolde

Since Chamonix was too small to have its own psychiatric hospital, Amélie Omont had been convalescing at a center in Annecy, about one hour away.

Drake turned, following the bright green sign leading them to the *centre hospitalier*.

Isolde shifted in her seat.

"Are you okay, Isolde?" he asked. "You don't have to do this."

Isolde shook her head. Two weeks had gone by since they'd agreed to the meeting. She couldn't lose her nerve now that the time had finally come. "I'm okay. I just ..."

"You heard what her doctor said yesterday." The

previous day, she and Drake had had a call with the doctor to prepare for the meeting. "If you feel uncomfortable at any point, we'll leave."

"I know, I know. I'm not worried ... or I am, but it's not about me. I want the meeting to go well, is all. There's a lot riding on it for Amélie."

Drake parked the car in the visitor's parking and together they walked towards the reception area. Although it was warm, she noticed he was wearing a long-sleeved blue shirt with the cuffs pulled down to his wrists.

Covering the scar.

Her heart skipped a beat.

"We're here to see Dr. Rubens," she said to the nurse behind the desk, hoping she had the name right.

The nurse nodded quickly. "The doctor is waiting for you. Please head down this corridor, room A5."

Isolde knocked on the door and opened it—her mouth slammed open in surprise. She didn't know what she'd expected, but it certainly wasn't to find Amélie Omont and an older man sitting calmly on two armchairs positioned next to an empty fireplace. She froze, staring at the comfortably appointed room, so different from the aseptic hallways behind.

Behind her, Drake cleared his throat, propelling her into action. Isolde took a step into the room.

The doctor stood up, holding a clipboard. "Ah, Dr. Durant. Lieutenant Jacobs. So glad you could make it.

Amélie and I were waiting for you. Please sit," he said, pointing to a sofa.

Amélie looked up at her with wide brown eyes. The woman had lost weight since the last time they'd met—and she'd been thin to begin with.

Isolde took a calm, steadying breath, calling on her professional training to relax.

"Amélie. How are you feeling?" Isolde asked.

Amélie stood up. "I'm sorry I hurt you," she said, including both Isolde and Drake in her apology. "I don't know what—" Her throat moved up and down as she swallowed compulsively. "No," she corrected herself. "It doesn't matter. I'm ... grateful that I didn't hurt you—or myself."

Isolde exchanged a quick look with Drake. Amélie's heartfelt apology had gotten to him as well.

Over the next half hour, Amélie's doctor led the conversation skillfully from the past to the present, and even got Amélie thinking about the future. Isolde and Drake discovered Amélie had been taking drugs to make her sleep for a long time, and weeks before the incident had started taking other drugs to make her more alert during the day. Though nobody was trying to excuse her actions, it was possible that the interaction between those two sets of drugs had precipitated the psychotic behavior they'd witnessed.

By the time they left the hospital, Isolde felt like she'd run a marathon—she was glad she'd done it, but felt physically and emotionally drained. They got back in the car in silence.

"I believed her," Drake said, sounding half surprised. "What did you think?"

"I believed her as well—and I have quite a bit of experience of people trying to lie to me."

He barked out a laugh. "I guess you do, Doc. I guess you do." He paused for a moment before continuing. "I wouldn't want to see her go to prison."

"She won't, not if you and I testify on her behalf."

Drake nodded. He now looked willing to entertain the possibility, which he hadn't been before. Isolde breathed a sigh of relief. As long as they could be certain Amélie wouldn't try to hurt anyone else, Isolde didn't want the woman punished too harshly—not after everything she'd already been through.

22

Isolde

Isolde watched Drake's thick forearms flex as he tightened the straps around the two mountain bikes strapped to the back of his SUV. She could still see the crisp, reddish outline of the fourteen stitches he'd gotten on his arm. It was healing well, but he'd probably always bear the scars.

The black T-shirt he was wearing highlighted the strength of his arms and pectorals. Isolde felt her mouth water as she thought of the muscles under that T-shirt. She wondered if they had time to go back inside for a quickie, or even if they should skip the bike ride completely.

She quickly pulled herself together. She'd been working long hours over the last weeks, and Drake had been incredibly patient with her. The only thing he'd asked of her was that she save this day to go mountain biking with him. He'd planned the outing meticulously, even going so far as to borrow a bike from Tess, Damien's wife, for Isolde to use. That was the smaller bike hanging from his car, which still looked huge to Isolde.

"I can't believe you've never been mountain biking. You're going to love it."

"Uh huh," Isolde said, noncommittally. She must have been twelve or thirteen years old the last time she'd been near a bike. She was willing to give it a fair shot, but wasn't as convinced about it as he was.

His use of the word *love* made her realize she still hadn't told him she loved him. But she did. She loved Drake. She loved him for his strength and his courage, for being willing to give them a second chance when she'd been too afraid. She might not have uttered the words yet, but she loved him enough to go out of her comfort zone, hence why she was standing outside her apartment at seven in the morning on a Saturday morning.

"Okay. We're ready." He smiled at her. "You look great."

Isolde's hand went self-consciously to her padded biking shorts, which made her ass look even larger than it already was.

Yeah, right.

Drake laughed. "You'll be glad for the padding in a bit."

"Take it easy on me, ok?" she asked, only half joking.

"I won't let anything happen to you," he promised. "Now come on, get in the car, I want to be there by eight."

Three hours later, Isolde could confirm two things: that she was very glad for the padding on her shorts, and that the best thing about mountain biking was riding behind Drake and getting to stare at his butt in those tight shorts he was wearing.

The jury was still out about mountain biking, as far as she was concerned. So far, she didn't know whether it was fun and exciting, or simply nerve-wracking and terrifying.

Drake turned his head to check on her. Although she couldn't see his eyes behind the sunglasses, his expression was more carefree and relaxed than she'd ever seen it before. Suddenly she was incredibly glad she'd come up here with him.

"You're doing great. Let's get up to that ridge and we'll stop for a picnic."

Music to my ears.

At the top of the ridge, Isolde dropped off her bike. She held on to Drake, her legs unsteady as those of a newborn colt. Her arm and leg muscles burned, partly from the exercise, but partly from how tense she'd been holding herself the whole time.

She took the water bottle he offered and drank gratefully.

"So, how am I *really* doing?" she asked.

He pulled her into his arms. He smelled of clean, male sweat. "I already told you. You're doing great. You haven't even made the mistake most rookies make, of pulling too hard on the brakes."

"How do you know?"

"You've yet to go over the bars," he deadpanned. "Sit down with me, Isolde," he said, bringing something large and colorful out of his backpack.

"Is that an actual picnic blanket?" The sight of the blanket in his hand was so incongruous, she couldn't help but laugh as he struggled to lay it out.

"What? Tess let me borrow it. I thought it'd be nice."

"It *is* nice. It's okay if I just collapse right onto it, right?" she asked, proceeding to do exactly that.

She closed her eyes, listening to the breeze over her head. It was one of those strange fall days that almost—though not quite—felt like summer again.

"Mmmm... you were right. This is amazing."

Moments later, Drake dropped onto the blanket next to her. She reached out to clasp his hand and pulled him on top of her. He kept his weight on his forearms to avoid crushing her, but she felt his lower body against her—felt the hard length that told her just how happy he was to see her.

"I'm not sure mountain biking together is such a good idea," he whispered in her ear.

"No?"

"I've had a hard-on the whole morning."

Her hand stroked down the length of his body. Drake hissed in a breath.

"I brought a light picnic for us, but we're not going to get to it if you keep doing that."

"What if I'm hungry for something else?" she asked, caressing the outline of his cock, surprised by her own forwardness. She'd never had sex outdoors before but, with Drake, for the first time in her life she felt safe to explore. She opened her eyes. "We *are* alone up here, right?"

"I've never seen anybody else up here," he confirmed, "and if someone were to come, we'd see them long before they saw us."

"Good," she said, licking her lips.

In reply, Drake pressed his mouth to hers, his touch soft but firm. Isolde opened her mouth, brushing her tongue against his lips, letting him know she wanted more. He took the hint, exploring the inside of her mouth with his tongue, the intensity building until the feel of his mouth on hers was the only thing that mattered in the world— and still she wanted more.

His hands went down to her breasts, caressing the soft globes. Her nipples rose to hard peaks.

Isolde moaned. "Drake ..."

"You drive me insane," he muttered. "Absolutely insane."

In a flurry of activity, they both shimmied out of their biking shorts. Following Drake's instructions, Isolde hadn't put on underwear under the shorts, so after a few instants of wriggling they found themselves naked below the waist.

"Are you sure nobody will see us?"

"I'm sure, but if it'll make you feel better ..." Drake grabbed the edge of the huge picnic blanket and draped it over them. "Let me see if I can't get you thinking about something else."

Moments later, his clever mouth on her pussy, she forgot to think of anything else. It was a long time before either of them remembered the picnic he'd packed for them.

Drake

"So, what was your favorite bit?" Drake asked later, as he strapped the bicycles to the bike rack once more. They'd both changed into a pair of jeans when they got back to the car—in his case, he'd foregone his boxer shorts and was going commando.

"Hmm... definitely the view up on that ridge," she teased.

He laughed. "I thought the view was pretty exquisite as well. We'll have to go back there soon."

Isolde dropped onto the SUV's seat. "Soon. But not today. I'm exhausted."

Drake looked at his watch to check on the distance. Maybe he'd pushed her too hard on the way down. "I know downhill rides can be stressful at first.

How about you come to my place, I'll run you a warm bath and cook some dinner?"

Isolde's eyes lit up at the thought. "Sounds like a plan."

He plugged his phone into the car charger. "Relax, we'll be there soon."

They were halfway into town when his phone rang. It was an unknown number. Drake put it on speaker.

"Jacobs," he said.

The phone line made a crackling noise, like there was faulty wiring.

"Hello?"

"*Monsieur* Jacobs? This is Jean Lepont. I'm the maintenance technician at the Brévent cable car," said an older voice.

"*Monsieur* Lepont. How can I help you?"

"I need to talk to you about something that happened the day of the accident."

Drake slowed down to take a curve. "I'm afraid I'm not directly involved in the investigation. I suggest—"

"One of the gendarmes gave me your number. I know you were there that day. Could you come see me?"

"Now?"

The crackling noise got louder. Drake put the call on hold and turned towards Isolde. "Is it okay if we stop by Brévent on our way back? It's a fifteen minute detour, more or less. But if you're tired, I can—"

Isolde nodded. "That's fine. I'll stay in the car and think of that warm bath."

"I can be there in twenty minutes, *Monsieur* Lepont."

Drake disconnected the call, wondering what the maintenance technician wanted to share with him. He remembered Hugo telling him the technician was highly experienced, with a proven track record.

He dialed Hugo's number, but his friend didn't pick up. By the time Drake parked outside the cable car mountain station, it was six p.m.—still light, though the sun was starting to grow dimmer. Behind the police tape, the building looked completely deserted.

"Wait here," he told Isolde. He put the keys to his car in her hand. "And lock the car doors behind me."

"You're scaring me, Drake. I thought you were just going to speak with the technician?" she asked, her honey eyes round with fear.

"I am," he said. "I'll be back in a few minutes. But, just in case, don't unlock the door for anyone who's not me. If I'm not back in fifteen minutes, you drive off and call Damien, okay?"

She held herself so rigidly, for a moment Drake was tempted to get back in the car and drive her home—then she nodded tersely and closed the car door. Drake heard the lock engage.

He stepped over the police tape designed to keep gawkers from approaching the cable car station until the investigation was through.

Drake pushed at the glass door, which was unlocked, and walked inside. He'd been here dozens of times, but never in the dark. He squinted while his eyes got used to the semi-darkness, looking for the light switch.

"*Monsieur* Lepont?" he said. His voice resounded loudly in the large, cavernous building.

He finally found the light switch but, when he pressed it, nothing happened.

Drake walked towards the large shadow of the cable car ahead, which took up a fair bit of the space. "*Monsieur* Lepont?" he repeated.

He tripped over something large lying on the ground. He righted himself quickly and touched the shape with the tip of his trainers. He swallowed hard, fishing for his phone, though he didn't need the light to know what it was he'd touched.

A body.

The man was lying face-down on the ground. He had long, gray hair, tied back in a ponytail. Drake kneeled beside the body and put his fingers to the man's neck, even though he already knew he was dead. Rigor mortis hadn't even begun to set in, though.

He hasn't been dead long.

Drake's next thought wasn't for the poor sap lying dead on the ground.

Isolde.

He had to get to her. Drake leaped to his feet. The movement caused something in his leg to tweak painfully— probably one of the multiple screws and plates holding his bones together. He ignored the pain, knowing the leg would hold.

Before he had a chance to take a single step, a figure appeared, standing between him and the exit. A large, bald man. Sweat glistened on top of his head.

Then the man looked up, and Drake recognized Alain Blanchard, the brother of the two victims.

His mind reeled.

What is he doing here?

"Blanchard?"

"Ah, you remember me, Jacobs." His gaze grew stony. "I certainly remember you."

"What's going on, Blanchard? Is this Jean Lepont?"

"It is. The bastard was trying to blackmail me, if you can believe that. He threatened to tell you everything he knew." Blanchard looked at the corpse behind them. "I thought we could reach an agreement, but when I got here, I heard him speaking with you. It sounds like his conscience got the best of him. Now he won't say anything."

"What is it you didn't want him to say?"

"My involvement in my brothers' accident, of course."

Fuck.

Drake looked down at his watch. He'd been inside for three minutes now.

Twelve minutes left until Isolde drives off and calls Damien.

218

He had to keep Blanchard engaged and talking for as long as possible.

Blanchard circled, moving closer, and Drake stepped around him. He didn't need to look back to know he was being herded towards the cable car gangway—there was no exit that way, but as long as they were moving away from the main road, where Isolde was waiting, Drake would comply. They were also moving closer to the large panoramic windows, so it was easier to see Blanchard now.

"I guess I have to kill you too," Blanchard said, bringing out a gun from inside his waistband.

Stupid way to carry a weapon.

Too bad he didn't blow off his balls.

Drake recognized the pistol. It was a PAMAS G1, one of the most common weapons in the country, used by the French Air Force, the Army and the Navy since the late nineties. He wondered how Blanchard had come across it.

And whether he knows how to use it.

"You deserve it, anyway, for meddling with my plans."

Drake backed another step. "You caused the accident on purpose? Why would you want to kill your brothers?"

"It's a long story—but I don't mind sharing it with you."

23

Isolde

Isolde had every intention of keeping her promise. She fiddled with the phone in her hands, confirming—for the fifth time in as many minutes—that cell phone reception was strong.

Ten minutes left.

Discomfort grew in the back of her mind. She struggled against it, telling herself Drake knew what he was doing. He was a member of the PGHM—he knew a lot more about this kind of situation than she did, and he'd asked her to stay put. If she went out now, she'd only be distracting him from his job.

Breathe, Isolde.

In and out.

In and out.

If Drake thinks there's no danger—

And then she realized what was wrong. If Drake hadn't been worried, if he'd seen no danger, he wouldn't have asked her to drive off and call Damien at the fifteen minute mark.

Making up her mind, Isolde picked up her phone again, scrolling down to Damien's contact. Before she could second-guess herself, she pressed the call button. Damien picked up on the second ring.

"Hello, Isolde? Is everything okay?"

She didn't bother with any pleasantries. "I need your help, Damien."

She proceeded to explain what had happened. As she got to the end of the story she faltered. "Drake asked me to wait before calling you, but I have a bad feeling—"

"Stay put, Isolde. Stay inside the car and lock the doors," Damien ordered, sounding a lot like Drake. "We're on our way."

"But Drake—"

"—can handle himself, Isolde. Wait for us inside the car. Please."

She hung up the phone, her eyes fixed on the doorway to the cable car hut. As the seconds passed and there was no word from Drake, Isolde's anxiety levels spiked. Her hand hesitated on the door handle.

I promised Drake I'd stay in the car.

He doesn't need your help, he needs his team's help.

But his team's not here—you are.

The feeling crystallized in her mind—if Drake

was in trouble, she was the only one who could help. She opened the door handle and got out of the car cautiously, closing the door behind her as quietly as possible. She shivered in the cool, evening air, glad she'd changed into jeans and a long-sleeve top but wishing she'd thought of bringing a sweatshirt as well.

Isolde stood behind the front door, listening for any sounds. If everything was okay, she'd head back to the car and—

The first voice she heard wasn't Drake's, and it wasn't one she immediately recognized. Though she couldn't understand the words, the tone sounded hostile.

I've heard that voice before ...

Isolde took a small step into the cavernous building—and saw Drake and a tall, round-faced bald man standing towards the far side of the room, where the cable car was waiting. The wind blew in from the mountain side, the noise making it impossible to understand the words the men were speaking.

But she didn't need to hear the words to notice how still Drake was holding himself. She looked to where he was staring—and saw the gun, pointed straight at Drake's chest.

Isolde's throat suddenly went dry. Her lungs seized, and her heart thundered inside her chest, loud enough to her own ears that she was surprised the men couldn't hear it.

She knew what was happening, of course—had

studied the body's reaction to fear in order to be able to better explain it to her patients. But *knowing it* and *feeling it* were two different things.

As the wind suddenly quieted down outside, Isolde heard Drake's voice, ringing out loud and clear. "You were willing to kill your brothers?"

The bald man shrugged. "It's not that difficult to understand. When our parents died, they left us a ruin of a company. In the last ten years, I've given everything to that company. I've made it into something great. And now my brothers, who've done nothing except spend the money *I* made, want to force me to sell."

Blanchard.

The brother of the two men injured in the cable car crash.

Isolde realized if Blanchard turned his head, he'd be able to see her clear as day. She ducked back behind the door. Falling to her knees was easy, they were shaking so hard—forcing air into her lung was harder. But she couldn't afford to lose her shit now.

She forced herself to take a deep, steadying breath, and cocked her head to better listen to what the two men were saying. Now that she couldn't see them, it was harder to make out what they were saying.

"You were behind the crash," Drake said.

"I'm good with machinery. I bribed Lepont to step out for a twenty-minute break and took care of things up here. It was meant to be a quick and painless death."

"But your brothers didn't die," Drake said calmly.

"Because of you, you bastard." There was real hatred in Blanchard's tone.

"Drop the gun, Blanchard. I'm a police officer. You're only making things worse for yourself," Drake said calmly.

"You underestimate me. I'm going to close this little episode tonight. It's going to be kind of prophetic, actually. The press will have a field day with it."

"If you shoot me—"

"I'm not going to shoot you. You're going to jump."

"I won't jump," Drake said, his voice deadly.

They were the same words Amélie had spoken—and they filled Isolde with fear the likes of which she'd never felt before. Her limbs shook so badly, she was glad she was already on the ground.

"If you don't jump," Blanchard's voice was almost pleasant at this point, "I'll take out both your kneecaps and push you off the ledge."

"You think that will help people believe I jumped?" Drake said, his voice dripping in irony. "You're insane, Blanchard."

Isolde forced more air into her lungs, trying to calm herself. Drake's team wouldn't get here fast enough. She had to come up with some way to help Drake. Her hand closed around a small, flat rock next to her left knee. Before she could second-guess herself, she threw it as hard as she could, towards the darkest corner of the cable car hut.

Blanchard's response was instantaneous. "What the hell is that?"

Drake

Drake's heart froze at the sound. He didn't dare look down at his watch, but knew there were still a few minutes to go from the original fifteen—which meant that noise could only have been made by one person.

She didn't wait in the car.

"What the hell is that?" Blanchard snarled, waving the gun in Drake's direction.

"That's my team," Drake bluffed, keeping his voice steady. "You didn't think I'd come alone, right? Now drop your weapon, Blanchard."

Blanchard laughed, a high-pitched, mirthless sound. "I have a genius IQ, Jacobs—and you, you're just a glorified lifeguard."

"Better that than a murderer," Drake deadpanned. Anything he could do to keep Blanchard's attention on himself, rather than on the origin of the sound, was effort well spent.

Please hide, Isolde.

"That's not your team. But you didn't come alone, didn't you? You brought that woman with you, the one you've been hanging out with."

He's been following us.

Blanchard sighed theatrically. "I can't have her running around talking about me. Get her to come out here."

Drake clamped his lips together. Nothing in the world could get him to call out to Isolde. Blanchard saw this and shrugged.

"Come out, dear, or I'll shoot out your boyfriend's kneecap. He won't be needing it soon, anyway. On three. One ..."

Breathe.

Isolde's smart.

"You're wasting your time. She's not here, Blanchard."

Blanchard ignored him. "Two."

It's okay.

She's had plenty of time to hide.

Blanchard's finger tightened imperceptibly on the trigger. Drake readied himself for the pain.

"Th—"

A movement from the entrance doorway had both men swiveling their heads. Isolde walked towards them, her hands up in the air.

"Don't hurt him."

Drake felt the room closing in on him.

Please, God, no.

I'll kill her myself if we survive this.

"Ah, there you are," Blanchard said. "Stand next to him. I want to see both of you."

"Isolde ..." Drake said.

She gave a small shrug. Her voice trembled. "I'm sorry, Drake, I couldn't stay in the car."

His heart almost broke at the dread in her voice.

Drake took a small step forward, positioning his body ahead of hers.

"Don't move a muscle, either of you." Sweat dripped down the side of Blanchard's face. The man wasn't as unaffected as he tried to appear. He brought out a handkerchief, struggling as a corner snagged on something in his pocket. For an instant, the barrel of the gun dropped slightly.

Knowing he wouldn't have a better chance, Drake leaped to the side. He pushed the green button that he knew would start the cable car.

Blanchard's mouth fell open. "What the hell are you—"

As the machinery throbbed and hummed its way to life, Drake grabbed Isolde by the shoulders and propelled her towards the open door of the now moving cable car, diving in after her.

A single shot rang out.

Drake felt the impact as a bullet entered his lower back. He scrambled towards the corner of the cabin, dragging Isolde with him, grateful his legs still worked.

The cabin door closed behind them as it started moving down the mountain.

Drake pushed Isolde onto the metal grating on the floor, covering her with his own body. He had no way of knowing how thick the frame and sides of the cabin were, but figured their survival was going to be more about luck than anything else. Four shots rang out in quick succession, striking the cabin's metal body.

So far so good.

Beneath him, Isolde trembled violently.

Drake wished he had his weapon with him. He wanted to inflict violence on Blanchard.

"Shhh," he said in a low voice. "Stay down, Isolde, it's going to be okay."

"I thought you said you'd never get into a cable car again," Isolde muttered.

Drake had to laugh. It was just like Isolde, to try to work through her fear, when most would huddle in a corner and weep. He was amazed at her strength.

"He's going to bring us back, isn't he?" she whispered, her expression grim again.

The green shadows of the trees below flew by, moving faster and faster. Drake heard a hissing sound from above.

No, he's not.

Whatever he did to the cable car last time, he's going to do it again.

He's going to cause another accident.

In his zeal to get Isolde away from the gun, Drake had played right into Blanchard's hand. If the cable car crashed, Blanchard could get rid of the technician's body, walk away, and never look back. Nobody would ever look at him for this.

"No. He's speeding it up," Drake said softly. He

would not lie to her. "He wants to cause another accident."

The heat in his back was quickly shifting to a high-pitched throbbing pain, but now wasn't the right time to worry about it. He could still move, and that's all that mattered.

"We're going to die, aren't we?" she said. Her hand sought his in a comforting grip. Drake realized she didn't want him to be scared.

She's thinks we're going to die, and she's trying to comfort me.

Drake stood up, bringing Isolde to her feet. He wrapped her hands around one of the metal poles designed for visitors to grab on to.

"What are we doing?" she asked.

"Grab on tight," he told her. "We're going to jump."

"Jump? Are you insane, Drake?"

Some piece of machinery above them hissed and cracked. Drake tried to remember whether that was the same sound he'd heard in the forest. Something inside him told him they didn't have long.

"Staying here is insane, Isolde. If we jump, we have a chance—" He hissed in pain. His back was turning into a ball of agony.

"Drake? What's wrong?" Isolde asked. Her hand came up to touch his face.

"Keep your hands on the pole," he said, ignoring her concern.

Drake made his way unsteadily to the door. His

strength was failing him—he needed to get it open now.

His fingers found a small crack in the door.

Bingo.

The muscles in his forearms tensed as he pulled, slowly opening a gap where he could fit first a hand, then a foot. He breathed a sigh of relief and pulled again, this time with a bit more leverage, cracking it open further. The wind rushed into the cable car.

"We need to get out right now."

Isolde whimpered.

"I'm scared."

"Listen to me. We're going to jump onto the next pylon. Together."

"No ..."

"The cable car has an automatic braking mechanism every time it approaches a pylon. It's designed to protect the machinery. We're going to use that," he said, with more certainty than he really felt. "You're going to hold on to me, just like that," he said, crouching so she could get onto his back.

He wished he had a harness and a carabiner—anything to clip her to him.

"You hold on to me and don't let go, Isolde—no matter what, okay?"

Her face was the color of chalk, but she nodded bravely.

"I'll hold on, Drake."

They were almost at the next pylon. Drake felt the cable car slow down almost imperceptibly.

Come on, slow down a bit more.

Drake crouched, waiting until the last possible instant before jumping. He let go of Isolde's legs, trusting her to hold on to him—he was going to need both arms free in order to grab on to the pylon.

For a long, horrifying instant, he thought he might not make it. The pylon stretched beyond his reach, and he realized he was moving too slowly, their combined weights pulling them down.

Drake grunted, stretching his arms towards the metal. If he missed, they'd drop thirty feet. The fingers of his left hand found the hand hold he needed but slipped. Drake rotated his body in the air, his right hand now the only thing that could stop them from plummeting to their deaths.

Still moving in what felt like slow motion, Drake prayed like he'd never done before. His right hand closed against the metallic hold, and he clamped his fingers around it.

Yes.

Isolde clung to his shoulders and neck. Her hold was tight, her breathing unsteady against his ear, but Drake knew she was doing her best not to choke him.

His left arm finally found the purchase it hadn't found before. For a moment, Drake hung there, his legs in a dead hang. His shoulder muscles strained. Drake groaned. He couldn't hold this position for long. He needed a foothold.

From his position, he could see the ladder that led all the way to the bottom of the pylon. To safety.

That's where you need to be.

Eight measly feet away.

Isolde's left arm slipped from his neck. She flailed, her hand poking his lower back as she struggled for purchase.

Drake saw stars. Black spots filled his vision. He was instants away from passing out.

Her fearful gasp brought him back from the edge. Her hand was back up by his neck.

"Drake? Were you *shot*?"

Her voice held a note of hysteria.

Drake clamped his jaw together—he couldn't afford to respond. He pushed the pain to the back of his mind. He ignored the cramping in his fingers, ignored everything except the ladder up ahead. The only thing that mattered was getting Isolde to safety.

Hand over hand, he began inching forward. His entire body shook with the effort. Time slowed to a crawl as he moved.

He felt Isolde's soft breath on his neck. It was exactly what he needed—a reminder that, if he passed out, they were both dead.

Keep going.

His muscles screaming in agony, Drake summoned every ounce of strength as he moved his hands forward along the bar. Finally, he was close enough to the ladder that he could twist his legs and put them against each side of the rung.

He exhaled in sharp relief. His arms and hands shook.

"Do you think you can climb down the ladder, Isolde?"

If she said no, he didn't know what he was going to do.

"Yes. Yes," she said quickly. "What should I do?"

"Lean over on my right side until you can grab onto the ladder. Don't let go with your left hand until you're sure you're stable."

Now that she knew he was hurt, she was careful to avoid his injury.

Thank God for that.

Drake felt her body shift sideways slowly. He released his right hand from the ladder to help her.

"Always three points of contact on the ladder," he told her.

"Okay. I suppose now's not the time to tell you, I'm not so fond of heights."

He laughed dryly.

"The ladder's too narrow for us to go together. I'll go first," he said.

"What if I fall?" she asked.

He didn't bother replying.

That's exactly why I'm going first.

"Follow right behind me."

Though he could hear her moving over his head, Drake looked up—he needed the visual confirmation. Thankfully, she seemed steady.

The way down seemed never-ending. The throbbing pain in his back had reached a crescendo—he gritted his teeth to the point of cracking and kept going.

Finally, he reached firm ground. As Isolde reached him, Drake put his large hands around her waist and brought her down to the ground safely with him.

"Thank God," she said. Her honey-colored eyes rounded in alarm as she looked at him. "Drake? You're hurt."

Until now he'd been holding on through sheer willpower, but now Drake felt his strength waning.

"Your back—" she stuttered. Her hands were shaking.

Drake went down on his knees in front of her. His hands found purchase on the grass beneath them.

"It's going to be okay," he whispered.

Suddenly, a couple bright lights illuminated the path from up the slope.

"They found us," Isolde said gratefully.

Drake's heart filled with fear. Those lights belonged to a quad. Damien and the team wouldn't have had time to—

Before he had a chance to warn Isolde, the vehicle came into view. His worst fears were confirmed when he saw Blanchard. The silence, as the man stopped the vehicle in front of them, was deafening.

Blanchard grabbed a dark object from the back of the quad. Drake wondered if he'd had time to reload.

"You just won't *die*," he said, his voice dripping in anger.

"Stay away from him," Isolde said angrily, placing herself in front of Drake.

Drake was torn between amazement at her courage and anger at Blanchard.

Fuck this.

Drake pushed himself to his feet. He swayed lightly, locking his knees together. He didn't need to be okay, he just needed to fool Blanchard into believing he was stronger than he actually was. Isolde turned around as if to help him but he warned her away with his eyes and took a step forward.

"Don't move," Blanchard said, swinging the gun towards him.

"Nobody is going to believe this was an accident, Blanchard," Drake said. "Let us go."

Blanchard considered for a moment.

"No. I can't do that. I'll figure out a way to dispose of your bodies."

Drake swallowed past his fear. There had to be something he could do to protect Isolde.

"Which one of you wants to go first?"

Isolde took her hand in his and squeezed his hand. He could feel her shaking, but her touch was strong. He squeezed back gently, trying to convey with this touch his love for her.

A tear rolled down her cheek.

I'm sorry, sweetheart.

"Let her go, Blanchard. She has nothing to do with this, she won't say anything," he begged. Isolde's hand tightened further.

"I'm not going anywhere without you," she said.

"Do you two think I'm stupid?" Blanchard asked. Anger mottled his face red.

I think you're a crazy, murdering asshole.

Drake looked head-on at the man. "I think you're insane if you don't realize my team will hunt you down for this."

"You go first, just so I don't have to listen to you anymore." Blanchard's finger tightened on the trigger. Drake looked head-on at the edge of the barrel, knowing he wouldn't see the bullet that ended his life.

In the silence of the forest, the sound of the bullet was deafening—then everything happened in a rush.

Damien, Jens and Hiro ran out from behind the trees, each holding a gun ahead of them. A red stain appeared on Blanchard's chest and he fell to the ground.

Damien ran over to kick Blanchard's gun away from him. The man wasn't moving.

"Are you okay?"

Drake staggered—with relief, this time.

Isolde tried to hold him, but Drake eased her hands off him. There was no way she could bear his weight. He went down on his knees hard.

"Drake!" she cried out, falling to her knees beside him. "Please help him!"

Jens was beside him in an instant, easing him down onto the ground. "Drake? Where are you hurt?"

"Blanchard shot him in the back," Isolde stuttered.

Jens pulled Drake's body towards him, raising his T-shirt. The doctor's look was grim.

"Bullet's still in there. Where's that ambulance, *Commandant*?"

"ETA five minutes," Damien replied. "Kat called them a while ago, just in case."

"Hold on, Drake," Jens said. "Help is on its way."

Drake found himself searching for Isolde.

"You okay?" he whispered.

"Please hold on, Drake. Don't leave me."

Drake nodded, feeling more relaxed than he ever remembered feeling. Even the pain was starting to fade. He started to close his eyes, then opened them again. There was one thing he needed to say to her, *au cas où*. Just in case.

"I love you, Isolde."

She brought her face close to his, her voice so low he had to strain to hear it. "You'd better live if you want to hear me say it back."

Drake laughed. Then his world went dark.

24

Isolde

Isolde sipped the lukewarm coffee Kat had brought for her. She'd counted the slats in the hospital waiting room ceiling a hundred times in the few hours they'd been here.

"Thank you," she said. Her shaking hand wrapped around the paper cup. If Kat noticed the tremors, she didn't say anything.

Isolde had traveled with Drake in the ambulance but, as soon as they'd gotten to the hospital, he'd been wheeled away into surgery. She hadn't been allowed to go in with him—none of them had, since it wasn't just her waiting out here. All his team members were there, as well as Tess, Damien's wife, who'd joined them later.

"He's going to be fine," Jens said, coming up beside her.

"You've spoken with the doctor?" she asked hopefully.

The tall man shook his head quickly, and she realized he didn't want to raise her hopes. "No, but I know Drake and he's a tough son of a bitch. He's going to be fine."

"I hope so," she said.

He has to be okay.

I haven't told him I love him yet.

"Has anybody taken a look at you, Isolde?" Damien asked, sitting beside her.

Isolde shook her head. "I'm fine." Her voice quivered in fear. She tried again. "I'm not hurt like Drake is."

Just then, the doors to the emergency room opened and Dr. Matthieu walked out.

Finally, a piece of good luck.

Isolde took a step forward.

"Dr. Matthieu," she said. "Robert."

"Isolde. Mr. Jacobs said you'd probably be out here."

Drake said ...

"He's talking? Does that mean—" Her tongue stuck to the roof of her mouth.

Dr. Matthieu nodded. His eyes were kind. He looked around, recognizing Drake's team. She could see the wheels turning in his mind, and the moment he decided it was okay to talk to them.

"The bullet grazed his kidney. We thought we might have to remove it, but finally we managed to contain the bleeding. He's still in the post-anesthesia care unit, but I expect him to make a full recovery."

Isolde felt herself sway in relief.

Kat was beside her in a second, placing an arm around her shoulder.

"Can I see him?" Isolde asked. She didn't care if she was cutting in front of his team. She needed to see Drake with her own eyes.

"He'll be moved to a room over the next hour." Dr. Matthieu looked at the tablet in his hand. "Room 212. Why don't you wait there?"

She nodded gratefully and thanked the doctor. After he'd gone back through the doors, Isolde turned to his team. They were all smiling from ear to ear. Gael and Hiro clapped each other in the back.

"See?" Jens said, his expression fierce. "I told you he was going to be okay."

Isolde hugged Kat.

"I was so scared, Kat, I was—"

"I know," Kat said.

"You probably think it's stupid. It's not like Drake and I—"

Kat's large blue eyes fixed on hers. "I recognize love when I see it, Isolde. You're in love with Drake. And I've known for a long time that he's in love with you."

"He thought he was dying when he said it," Isolde said uncertainly. "We'll have to see how he feels—"

"I know Drake, Isolde. That has nothing to do with it."

Isolde looked up at Damien. "Do you want to wait for him in the room?" she asked, knowing how close Drake and Damien were.

"And disappoint him?" Damien shook his head. "You go on up, Isolde. Tell him we'll be back to see him later today."

"Are you sure?" she asked, amazed at how badly she needed this.

Damien nodded. "Of course. You'll call us if there's any change, or if you need anything?"

Isolde nodded, her expression serious.

"Thank you," she told them. "I'll let Drake know you were all here."

A few minutes later, she found herself in room 212. The walls in this floor were the palest yellow, a color that somebody must have found cheerful years earlier but that hadn't aged well. She walked past the empty space where the bed would go and opened the curtains before realizing it was night-time.

Nothing to see.

She allowed herself to collapse into the plasticky-looking armchair. Placing her hands on her knees to steady herself, she took a couple deep breaths to calm herself.

She'd told everyone she was okay, that she didn't need to see a doctor—and it was true Blanchard hadn't touched her. But, while she might physically be okay, the stress and fear of the last hours had taken a toll on her.

She thought back to the moment when her hand had touched Drake's bloody back. She knew what it'd cost him to take them to safety—knew also that he would have given his life for her if necessary. Just like she would have done anything to save him.

She wasn't sure whether it was minutes or hours later that the door opened and a nurse and an orderly wheeled in the bed carrying Drake. Drake's eyes were closed, his normally golden skin pale against the crisp white bed clothes.

Isolde rose quickly, then stood around with nothing to do while the nurse positioned the bed in the right place.

"If he needs anything, press this button and I'll come right over," she told Isolde. The nurse's shoes made no sound as she left the room, closing the door behind her.

Isolde was about to sit down again when Drake opened his eyes.

"You're here," he whispered.

"Drake." Her eyes filled with tears.

"Hey. Why are you crying?" he asked.

"I'm not crying," she said, wiping her hand over her eyes. "I'm just happy."

Drake brought up the hand that wasn't trapped by the IV.

"Come here."

She pulled the arm chair closer to the bed and gave him her hand.

"I was so scared, Drake."

"I told you everything was going to be fine."

"That's what people say when they think they're going to die."

He considered that for a moment. "Is it? Well, I'm not going to die."

He licked his lips. They looked painfully dry.

"Would you like an ice cube, to suck on?" she asked. The nurse had left some on a small table.

He nodded gratefully.

"Is Blanchard ..."

"He's dead," she said. "His brothers came over to identify the body. They were ... distraught."

"He fooled us. He fooled everyone." Drake settled back down on the bed. "You look tired, Isolde. You should go home and get some rest."

She opened her mouth, suddenly feeling self-conscious. "I'm staying," she said. "Unless you don't want me to stay, of course. If you'd prefer for me to call—"

His hand squeezed hers gently. "Stay, please. I'll sleep better knowing you're here, and safe."

"We're both safe, Drake," she said.

And I love you.

But she didn't say that last part out loud.

Drake was asleep a couple minutes later.

Isolde found an extra blanket in the closet and settled into the armchair. Her eyes had barely closed when she woke up again. At first she didn't hear anything, so she didn't know why she was awake. Then she heard Drake's unsteady breathing. She turned towards him, looking for his hand.

"Drake? Are you okay? Are you in pain?"

Tears filled his gray eyes—in the dim hospital lighting, they looked tortured.

"Thank God you're safe. It was just a nightmare," he said, as much to convince himself as her.

"I'm fine," she said. "Thanks to you."

She'd never forget the way he'd stepped in front of her—gotten shot to protect her, and then managed to get her to safety.

"So ... when do I get to hear it?"

"Hear it?" she repeated, confused.

"You said I'd have to live to hear you say it."

"You remember that?"

"I remember every instant we spend together, Isolde."

"I ... I love you, Drake," she said quietly, baring her soul to him.

This time he was the one who took her hand in his and squeezed gently.

"I love you too, Isolde. More than life itself."

25

Isolde

"Congratulations, Tess!" said a chorus of voices. The entire Chamonix PGHM, as well as several other friends, had come out tonight to celebrate Tess's success.

Tess blushed prettily.

"So, when can we read it?"

"Where can we buy it?"

Tess looked around her, laughing. Isolde knew the woman well enough by now to know she was proud, happy, but also more than a bit uncomfortable at being shoved into the limelight.

"Let her breathe, everyone," she said. Tess shot her a grateful look. "She'll tell us all about it."

"My agent found a publisher who's interested in

the book, but there's still a lot of work to be done before it gets to the bookstores. To answer your question, it probably won't be in bookstores until next summer."

Gael's face dropped. "That's a long time."

Isolde knew Tess was downplaying her success. She'd only finished the book a couple months ago, and already a publisher was willing to take it and offering her a handsome advance for it.

"Maybe I can get you an early copy," Tess said, laughing.

"And start writing the next one," the coffee shop owner interrupted. Isolde knew, from speaking with Tess, that this was the place where Tess had written a significant part of the novel, while Damien's son was in school or summer camp, so it seemed fitting that this would also be the place to celebrate the success.

Isolde looked around, hardly recognizing the place where she often grabbed a cup of coffee on her way to work. The space had been transformed for tonight's event. Amber lights hanging from the ceiling contributed to creating a warm, sultry feeling, showcasing the breathtaking view of Mont Blanc out the large picture window.

"To the next one!"

They all brought their glasses together. The champagne flowed.

"I am so proud of you, honey," said Damien. Love shone in his eyes as he looked at his wife.

"Even if I have to wait, I can't wait to read it," Gael said, raising his glass.

"When was the last time you read a novel, Gael?" Kat teased. Her eyes sparkled good naturedly.

"I've seen some books in his place," Hiro stepped in, keeping the peace.

"You've been to his place?" Kat asked. Her eyes narrowed. "Why haven't the rest of us been invited?"

Isolde listened to them, enjoying their easy banter. It was easy to see why they made such a great team together.

"Congratulations, Tess," Drake said. He was sitting a table just a few feet away. His powerful legs, encased in those tight jeans, looked strong, but the fact that he was sitting down told her everything she needed to know.

He's nowhere near his full strength.

He'd insisted on coming out to the party after being discharged from the hospital just hours earlier. Isolde felt sick to her stomach when she thought of how close they'd both come to dying. If his team hadn't arrived when they did—

"I should probably go home," Isolde said. She hesitated for a moment.

Drake was on his feet in an instant. "Are you feeling alright?"

Isolde clenched her jaw to stop herself from sniping at him.

He's the one who was hurt, and he's treating me with kid gloves.

"I'm fine."

"Could you come outside with me for a minute before leaving?"

She nodded. "Of course."

Drake moved towards the exit, his gait cautious and stiff.

"What is it?" she asked.

"There's something I need to tell you, and I don't want the others to hear."

She stood awkwardly in front of him. "Are you okay?" She realized, suddenly, how pale he was.

What if there's something wrong. What if his kidney—

Drake shook his head, licking his very dry lips. "I'm fine."

Isolde wanted to kiss those lips. She closed her eyes against the image. She needed to focus on what he was saying, not stand here outside the bar with some kind of sex scene running through her mind.

Except Drake wasn't speaking, and he wasn't even there anymore.

Isolde started when she saw him go down on his knees. She dropped quickly beside him.

"Drake! Oh my God, I'll go get—"

Belatedly, she realized he hadn't gone to his knees. He'd gone to *one* knee.

What?

His next words were quiet. "Will you marry me, Isolde?"

He was holding something in his hand—a small, glittering object.

"What is that?"

He looked up at her, then down at the ring. It looked minuscule in his tough, calloused palm.

"It's a ring."

"I can see it's a ring."

He cleared his throat.

"I bought it this morning, after leaving the hospital. But if you don't like it, we can—"

She liked it. Loved it, even. And she hadn't even gotten a proper look at it.

"I love it," she said. "And I love you."

"Wait," Drake said. "Does that mean your answer is yes?"

Isolde nodded. Happy tears threatened to fall, but she wiped them angrily away. She cupped his cheek gently. They were both still on their knees when the door to the coffee shop opened and somebody stepped outside.

"What are you guys doing—" That was Kat's voice. "Oh man, hurry up and kiss her, because I'm going to tell the others!"

Three minutes later, there were more people outside the coffee shop than inside. By then, Drake and Isolde were both standing, his arm draped protectively over her shoulder.

Gael and Jens whistled sharply.

"About time, Drake," Damien said, clapping him on the back—hard.

Isolde glared at him.

"Have you set a date already?" Hiro asked. Isolde was starting to shake her head no, when Drake interrupted.

"Soon." Drake went on to explain himself. "We've wasted enough time. Isolde said yes, and we're going to do this soon."

Isolde nodded, holding on to Drake's hand. He was strong and solid—he looked like nothing could fell him, but she knew how close she'd been to losing him just a few days earlier. None of them knew how long they had in this world, and they weren't going to let one more second slip away.

"Drake, Isolde, *félicitations*," Kat said, very formally, but her eyes were twinkling with happiness.

Isolde's heart filled with joy as she took in the love that each team member had for Drake. They were a family. She knew they were going to have to speak to the colonel again, now that her relationship with Drake has progressed further. They'd figure it out, together, like they had everything else. For tonight, she basked in the love that they shared.

Kat's phone rang shrilly. The pilot raised her hand in apology and moved away from the group to answer. They were all so busy planning the wedding already, Isolde was the only one who saw the expression on Kat's face as she listened to whoever was speaking on the other side. For a moment, Isolde could have sworn that was fear etched on the woman's voice. A moment later, the lines smoothed away—by the time she ended the call a few seconds later, Kat was smiling again.

"Is everything okay, Kat?" Isolde asked quietly as the woman moved back towards the group.

Kat looked at the phone in her hand, as if expecting it to ring again any second.

"Yeah, everything's fine. It's all fine."

Isolde suddenly found herself engulfed in Drake's embrace. She hung on to his huge biceps for support, feeling his strength and power.

"What do you say we do it next week?" he asked. At her quizzical look, he clarified. "Get married, I mean."

"Uh ... next week? I don't know, Drake, I'm going to have to look at my work calendar and ..."

He pondered that for a second. "This is a busy time of year for us as well. We can delay the honeymoon until after the winter season. But I don't want to wait until then to marry."

His look was so hopeful, Isolde didn't want to disappoint him—plus, she needed him to understand just how much she wanted to marry him. "Okay. Next week it is."

She hardly heard the cheers around them, caught as she was in Drake's smile.

It was a while until they were alone again. Most people had gone inside to get another drink. "You still want to head home?" he asked.

"I want to go home with you," she said, holding on to his hand.

"I have something for you first, though," he said awkwardly.

"You do?" she asked, surprised. "You didn't need to get me anything. You already got me a ring."

"I planned this some time ago. It just wasn't ready until tonight."

Out of his jacket pocket he brought out a small, flat, package, around the size of a postcard. She opened it, curious to see what was inside, and found herself staring at a beautiful framed painting. It was an exact rendition of her car, down to the tiniest scratches on its side.

She looked up in surprise.

"Drake, it's beautiful," she said. "I love it. It's exactly my car."

"Good, because I'd like you to keep this one—" Drake pulled in a deep breath, "and get rid of the other one."

"Get rid of my car?" she asked, laughing. "And what am I supposed to drive to work tomorrow?"

"This one," he said, activating the key fob in his pocket. One of the cars parked on the street in front of the coffee shop lit up. It was an SUV, exactly the same as his but dark blue. Isolde looked up in surprise.

"It's yours," Drake said.

"Are you crazy? You can't just go around giving people cars."

"Technically you're not *people*—you're my fiancée," he said. "But I wanted you to have the car, anyway. It just took a while for it to get here."

She started to speak, but he held on to both her hands in one of his larger ones.

"Hear me out, please, Isolde. I know so many things are outside our control. I'm learning to live with that. But I can't live, I can't breathe, knowing you're not being as safe as possible."

She clutched the beautiful painting to her chest, nodding. He was right. It was time.

"Okay. Tomorrow I'll go get this framed. And we can sell my car."

"Thank you," he whispered. "I love you."

"I love you too. And I promise I'll take good care of the car," she said, bringing his head down for a kiss.

-- -- -- -- -- -- --

Read on for a taste of
Mont Blanc Rescue Book 3...

PREVIEW: MONT BLANC RESCUE
BOOK 3

Kat

Kat's skis cut effortlessly through the fresh powder.

Although the Chamonix Mont Blanc Valley resort had officially opened in early December, the snow had been mediocre at best throughout the holidays. Last night's snowfall, the first of the new year, marked the real start of what was set to be a great ski season.

She wasn't the only one who'd had the idea of coming up here today. At the top of the cable car, she'd had to step around a crowd of eager skiers and snowboarders who'd stopped to stare at the Glacier d'Argentiere. Unlike them, however, Kat wasn't here to admire the view.

As a member of the *Peloton de Gendarmerie de Haute Montagne*, Mont Blanc's Search & Rescue team,

Kat had combed through every run in the resort, and knew exactly where to go to escape the crowds.

She leaned hard into her skis, aiming for the narrow left-hand track that led down to Pylones, her favorite black run. It was a long, steep, exhausting run—Kat and her team had come up here more than once to rescue skiers who'd overestimated their abilities. Today, with all the fresh snow, it was going to be exactly what she needed to forget her worries.

A small voice inside her suggested maybe today wasn't the best day to ski a black run alone. Normally, Kat would have checked to see who else from the team was off, and maybe made it a group ski session. Today, however, she'd needed to be alone. She was still shaky from the news she'd received and needed time to process.

Jacques is back in town.

In all fairness, she should have expected he'd come back at some point. Jacques Peres was a Chamonix-born-and-bred snowboarder, and even though he'd been living in the United States for the past ten years, every time he won a new medal or award, the town filled with the news of his victories. It was enough to make her want to throw up every time she saw his picture on the local news—though not half as bad as when she'd heard, just weeks earlier, that he'd be back in town for the Victory Games that would take place on January tenth.

Now, all Kat wanted was for the games to be over and for Jacques to leave once again.

Please let him leave quickly.

He can't stay.

I've made my life here.

It was hard to recall the violence Jacques had inflicted on her. She'd been nineteen years old and had worshipped the ground he walked on. By the time she'd finally gotten the courage to speak up, nobody had believed her. That had hurt almost as much as the psychological and physical violence that Jacques had inflicted on her.

She'd been lucky he'd left town, and she'd had a chance to rebuild her life. She'd joined the gendarmerie, had eventually become a rescue pilot, and had made a great life for herself. She now had a career she loved, great friends, almost everything she'd ever wanted—and yet the thought of seeing Jacques again made her feel like the lonely teenager she'd once been.

She shook her head under the bright yellow PGHM-issued helmet she was wearing. Although she was off duty and was wearing a bright red ski suit instead of her dark blue and black PGHM ski uniform, she didn't own any other helmets, and wouldn't consider hitting the slopes without one.

The north-facing slope meant it was always chilly up here. The frigid mountain air went straight into her lungs as she inhaled, relaxing her.

She couldn't help smiling as she caught sight of the first moguls, just as the run became steeper. She was glad she'd had her skis professionally serviced just weeks earlier—she'd be needing those sharp edges now.

She rotated easily between the bumps, keeping her upper body steady and letting her legs act like a suspension system. Instead of stopping at the end of the mogul field, she went straight into the steeper section of the black run, executing several smooth, short turns right down the fall line. Her skis ate into the steep, narrow terrain naturally.

She was still smiling as she caught sight of a slight figure—he looked like a boy—barreling towards her. He looked nowhere near confident enough on skis to be on this run.

Turn. Turn.

The boy missed the turn. Kat pushed hard on her edges to avoid him—just in time to see another skier appear on her other side. The second skier whooped excitedly, seemingly unaware of the danger.

Shit.

They're going to make a sandwich of me.

She turned hard, angling her skis towards the edge of the piste, narrowly avoiding the second skier, only to see a third, larger figure sitting on the side of the piste, staring intently at something in his hands.

Oh no.

Kat knew she couldn't avoid him, but she dropped her poles and threw herself onto the snow in an attempt to slow herself down before she hit the man. She felt a sharp jab on her ribs and her hip—suddenly, the fresh powder snow didn't feel that soft.

As she slid inexorably towards the man, the world went into slow motion. She caught sight of impossibly blue eyes and strong arms that opened wide to meet her onslaught.

She hit his body hard, and even though she pressed herself against the side of the mountain, the slope was too steep and there was no chance to stop their fall.

They rolled down the slope in a tangle of arms and legs. His arms went around her in a protective hug. Her elbow found somewhere soft. She heard a sharp intake of breath, but the man didn't release his hold.

Finally, all movement stopped, and the world was silent once again. Silent, and impossibly bright. She realized her goggles were gone. She was also cold all over, her suit having collected a shovelful of snow inside the neckline.

The arms surrounding her body opened up, and Kat raised her head, blinking a few times to dispel the dizziness. When her eyes finally focused, she found herself staring into eyes the color of a cloudless summer sky.

I didn't make up that color.

She was also lying right on top of the owner of the eyes.

"Fuck."

At first, because it was the same word that was echoing around in her mind, she didn't realize it was the man speaking.

"Are you okay?" he asked, his voice deep and husky. He sounded surprisingly calm.

Kat took a moment to look at him. He was wearing a helmet, thank goodness. His goggles had slipped to around his neck. Below the black helmet, his face was clean-shaven, with a strong nose and chiseled jaw. A bruise was starting to show on his cheekbone, probably from when some part of her anatomy had struck him.

He was one of the more handsome men she'd ever set eyes on, and that was before even considering those clear, blue eyes, currently shining straight at her.

Kat swallowed, her throat suddenly dry.

"I'm the one who should be asking," she said. "I'm on top of you."

His mouth curved into a wry smile, and it suddenly seemed to Kat that tumbling halfway down a black run might have been worth it just to see the way the smile lit up his face.

"That you are," he said, making no attempt to move.

She stared at him a moment longer, then realized he couldn't move, of course, not with her on top of him. She was making a fool of herself.

"Let me move out of your way," she said, embarrassed. She rolled off him carefully, looking around them. They'd ended up in a shallow part of the slope, close to the trees lining the side of the piste. Below them, the black run continued, steep and bumpy.

Thankfully, the run above them looked empty, but Kat knew that could change quickly. This wasn't a good place to sit around.

"What were you doing—" She stopped as he arched his brow. She tried again. "Let me start again. I'm sorry. I know *I'm* the one who ran *you* over."

He shrugged, and raised himself on his elbows, digging his elbows in, his hands up behind him. "It's okay. I saw what those reckless teenagers were doing. You made the right choice."

"Are you sure you're okay?" she asked. Something about the way he was holding himself struck her as odd. "Can you stand up?"

He shook his head. "No. I can't," he said straightforwardly, his voice still very calm.

Shit.

Don't panic. This is what you do on a daily basis.

This is just like any other rescue.

Except it wasn't. The thought of this man being hurt—the thought that she'd been the one to hurt him, made tears spring to her eyes. She rubbed at them angrily.

With shaking hands, she went looking in her ski suit pocket for the radio she always carried with her. She realized as she stared at the radio in her hand that she'd lost a glove during the fall.

"Hey, hold on," the man said, but she ignored him, bringing her naked hand to her mouth. Although her heart was beating fast, she spoke clearly and calmly into the radio.

"This is Kat Barreau, from the PGHM. I'm two thirds of the way down Pylones. There's been a crash. One male victim." She took a deep breath. "Likely back injury."

She held her breath until the reply came. "Kat? This is Jens. Drake and I are ten minutes away. We'll bring the stretcher."

Kat sighed in relief. Jens was a doctor. The stranger couldn't be in better hands.

"Copy. Please hurry." The stretcher might prove an uncomfortable ride, but it'd be the quickest way of getting him down. She wished she had her helicopter, so she could get him to a hospital even faster.

Her hands still shaking, she put the radio back in her pocket and reached back towards the man. If she weren't wearing a one-piece suit she'd take the jacket off and cover him with it—anything to make him more comfortable.

"You're with Search & Rescue?" he asked. He didn't sound like he was in pain. "Call your colleagues back and tell them not to bother. The good news is, I couldn't stand five minutes ago either."

Her mouth fell open in shock.

"What?"

For a moment, she wondered if he'd hit his head during the fall. Then she noticed something she should have noticed earlier, except she'd been too busy staring into his bright blue eyes. The man wasn't wearing ski or snowboarding boots. His boots were sturdy, waterproof boots—the kind of boots worn for hiking. And, although the tops looked scuffed, the soles looked brand new.

Her eyes went higher—under the black ski pants, his legs looked slighter than she would have expected for someone with such a muscular upper body.

He nodded, pointing up the slope, around the spot where he'd been sitting.

A sit ski.

Hell.

I just ran over a disabled skier.

She recovered quickly, clearing her throat.

"Okay. Are you hurt anywhere else?"

"I think I'm okay, but I'll probably need to get checked out by a doctor anyway," he said honestly, "since I can't feel anything below my hips."

"Shit."

"Yeah," he agreed.

Kat blushed. "I'm sorry. I didn't mean to say that out loud. And I'm sorry I ran you over."

"You say that word a lot. It's okay. Cancel the radio help. I'll see a doctor later. No need to get your colleagues to come all the way up here."

She nodded and took a deep breath before calling Jens on his mobile. She didn't go into details, just cancelled her earlier request and pocketed the radio once again. She turned to the man again.

"I'm glad I didn't hurt you, actually. It would have been a real black mark on me if I had," she said, allowing herself a small smile.

"Because you're with the *Peloton de Gendarmerie de*

Haute Montagne. Of course." He laughed, then, and if she'd thought his smile was beautiful before, the laugh made something inside her clench. "I'm Luc Fournier, by the way. Are *you* okay? You took quite a fall. I saw how you threw yourself down to try to avoid me."

Now that he mentioned it, Kat's ribs and hips were killing her. But she knew the difference between a bruise and an actual injury, and this was definitely the former.

He looked worried, so she nodded quickly.

"Nice to meet you, Luc. I'm Kat Barreau."

He tested the name softly. She liked the way he said it. "Kat. Is that for Kathérine? Katrina?"

She blushed.

Try Hekate.

"I'll tell you this much for now: my parents had a sense of humor."

"Ah, a challenge," he said, nodding. "I like that." He shifted his weight on his elbows.

"Are you okay? How can I help?" she asked.

"You can grab my sit ski for me. It'll take me a while to drag myself up there if I have to do it on my own."

Kat blushed for the third time in as many minutes, and set out to do exactly that, determined also to find her missing goggles and glove.

Luc

Luc watched the woman as she made her way easily up the steep slope.

From his prone position, the view was spectacular. He indulged himself for a few moments. She had great legs, and an amazing ass. Red curls fell down her back—he'd always loved redheads. But it was her dark blue eyes which had caught his attention first—he'd been lost the instant she'd looked up at him.

Stunning.

He felt an unusual pressure around his groin area.

Down, boy.

He rarely had reason to talk to his penis anymore, and it wasn't like the erections he got where that useful anyway, since they usually went away long before he had the chance to do anything about them.

He let out the breath he'd been holding and watched as she picked up her poles and skis, placed them by his sit ski, then walked around, looking around for something.

Luc wished he could help search for whatever it was she was looking for.

Or do anything else, other than lie here like a lump.

He shook his head to clear the thought. He knew from experience only madness lay down that road.

Moments later, she turned back to look at him, waving a small blue object in her hand—a glove. She was smiling widely as she clicked her boots in place and skied her way easily towards him. Even though she was burdened by his sit ski, which he knew weighed a ton, she was a graceful skier.

Luc sat up, using his arms to straighten his useless legs in front of him.

She came up beside him and executed a flawless stop. She rubbed her hands together, now wearing both gloves.

"I didn't find my goggles, but I found my missing glove," she said, smiling. "Brrr ... it's cold."

Luc nodded his agreement. His neck and arms felt cold. He was never sure how his legs were going to feel—sometimes, on warm days, they'd feel cold, then on a cold day they'd feel too warm. Or even, one leg would feel cold and the other one would feel warm. It was one of those fun facts about spinal cord injuries that nobody ever bothered to tell you about.

"What are these called?" she asked, pointing to his poles, which had short ski blades on the end.

"Outriggers. I use them to balance, and to help me push."

She nodded. "What were you doing up there, anyway?"

"I thought there was something wrong with my suspension, and stopped to take a quick look. Maybe not the cleverest idea, now that I think about it."

"Do you always ski alone? Isn't that dangerous?"

His lip curled up in a small smile. "No more dangerous than for you, I'd imagine. Though I *am* going to have more trouble getting going again," he added mournfully.

She used her pole to release her ski bindings, then kneeled down beside him.

"I'll help," she said, then quickly corrected herself. "How *can* I help?"

Luc appreciated the fact that she didn't try to grab him, or tell him what they should do. He got the feeling she hadn't had any personal experience with disabilities, but that she was trying to make up for her lack of knowledge with kindness and common sense.

He smiled what he hoped was an encouraging smile.

"Could you grab the sit ski and place it next to me? Like that. Thanks."

"Now what?" she asked.

"I've got this," he said. "I'm just going to need you to hold the ski in place so it doesn't slide around."

Luc lifted his legs, putting his boots together to help him. With his right hand, he grabbed onto the side of the sit ski frame. He made a fist with his left hand, readying himself. Then, trusting her to keep the sit ski stable—and knowing he'd end up flat on his face if she didn't—he pressed his fist hard against the ground, using it to propel himself upwards. In one swift move, he pulled himself straight up and onto the bucket seat.

"That's pretty impressive," she said.

Despite Luc's upper body strength, this move only

worked because he was six-two, but he didn't bother explaining that to her.

It'd taken him a fair amount of work to get his upper body strong enough to make up for what his lower body couldn't do anymore but now, six years after the accident, there wasn't much he couldn't do. He was glad his doctors at the rehabilitation center had pushed him. Without them, it might not have occurred to Luc that he could transfer from his wheelchair to a sit ski, a snowmobile, a snowcat, or any other kind of vehicle—that just because he was paraplegic didn't mean he had to sit still.

He took a minute to rearrange his legs and tie himself into the seat before pulling the outrigger straps through his wrists.

"There. I'm ready," he confirmed, signaling that she could let go.

She didn't look at him as she stepped back into her skis.

"I'll follow you down," she said in a carefully neutral voice.

Luc didn't bother hiding his smile this time around.

"Are you worried I won't be able to get down?" he asked.

"I'm sure you're a good skier. I just want to make sure you're okay," she said.

It was touching, actually. And a part of him welcomed the chance to show off a bit.

Snow was Luc's friend. Anywhere the ground was

white, he could go, and he could go fast. He took off without waiting for her to finish getting ready. He'd already seen her ski, and knew she'd have no trouble catching up.

His ski ate up the whiteness in front of him. That was one of the things he loved about the sport: skiing was the great equalizer. It didn't matter if the ski was under him or under someone who could walk, it would turn exactly the same way.

Luc was grateful his injury hadn't affected his ability to control his abdominal and lumbar extensor muscles, as this had allowed him to develop a more aggressive and effective skiing strategy than might otherwise have been possible.

He leaned deeply into the turn, edging his ski into the soft powder. If there was one thing Luc knew, was how to turn a steep gradient to his advantage.

Not that different from snowboarding.

The thought made him smile. Before his accident, Luc had been one of those snowboarders who looked down their nose at skiers. Now, he just felt lucky he could ski at all.

He didn't stop until he'd reached the bottom of the Les Grands Montets cable car. Then he turned, unsurprised to find Kat right behind him.

"Damn," she said, stopping far enough from him to avoid spraying him with snow. "I'm embarrassed now. You should have stayed behind to make sure *I* was okay."

Luc laughed. Skiing was what he did best in life.

That and snow grooming, which he'd been doing for the last five years in a Swiss ski resort, before coming over to Chamonix. But snow grooming was a job. Skiing was ... his life.

She took off her helmet, and Luc went breathless. She was even more beautiful than he'd figured.

While he struggled to regain speech, Kat reached over and picked something off his hair. The gesture, innocent as it was, made Luc shiver. He'd become much more sensitive to people touching him since the accident—perhaps because it didn't happen as often anymore.

Electricity crackled between them. He watched her pale throat move up and down several times—she'd felt it as well.

"Would you ... would you like to grab a cup of coffee together? Least I could do, since I ran you over."

Six years earlier, he would have jumped at that offer. Now, not so much.

Not that any of this was her fault.

Luc frowned. "I'm not going to sue you or the town, you know? You don't owe me anything."

She moved back as if he'd slapped her. "No. That's not what I ..."

He realized he was being an asshole—which surprised him. He considered himself a friendly guy. At least, he normally didn't have any trouble *not* being an asshole.

Luc took off his helmet and placed it on the floor next to him, considering his next words.

"I'm sorry. I know what you meant."

"Okay," she said. Her smile came back, though it was more tentative this time around.

She's interested.

Please tell me it's not the wheelchair she finds interesting.

Since his injury, Luc had met a few women who got turned on by the wheelchair, or, he supposed, by the idea of taking care of someone else. But he'd worked hard to become one hundred percent independent, hadn't needed any help since the moment he'd left the rehabilitation clinic five months after his accident, and wasn't about to spend time with someone who considered his inability to walk to be his most attractive trait.

"Where did you learn to ski?" she asked.

"I used to be a snowboarder," he said, leaving out the fact that he'd won the Snowboard World Cup twice. It seemed like that had happened a lifetime ago. "I didn't start skiing until after my accident," he added cautiously.

He expected a well-meant *I'm sorry*, perhaps a question about the accident. People were naturally curious about it. But she surprised him once again.

"You're an athlete," she said, her expression shutting down. She suddenly looked like she couldn't wait to get away from him. "You're here for the Victory Games, aren't you?"

Luc was about to reply when two men appeared, both of them dressed in black and blue PGHM ski uniforms.

"Everything okay, Kat?" the tall, blond man asked, looking curiously at Luc.

"Everything's fine. Jens, Drake, meet Luc Fournier."

Both men nodded politely at him. "We were nearby, so thought we'd come check on you."

"Thanks. We thought we might need help, but everything was okay in the end."

"We'll go on our way, then. Don't forget Damien has called a team meeting tomorrow at eight. Nice to meet you, Luc."

Kat waved them away. She ran her fingers through her red curls, trying unsuccessfully to smooth them into submission.

"You work with them?"

"Yeah," she said. "I'm a search & rescue pilot." The pride in her voice was evident.

Damn.

She's so out of your league, it's not even funny.

But she wanted to have coffee together. Maybe you should take her up on that offer.

He never had a chance to open his mouth.

"I have to go," she said, her expression guarded once again.

You missed your chance, buddy.

"Sure. I should go get my chair back before the

lifts close. The lift attendant is holding it for me. I'll see you around, maybe?"

Kat nodded, but her attention was clearly elsewhere. Luc already missed her sunny smile.

As he pushed off, Luc noticed a tall, slim snowboarder approaching her. An enormous smile stretched the man's face, his teeth bright against deeply suntanned skin.

Luc groaned under his breath.

ACKNOWLEDGMENTS

To you, the reader, thank you for joining me in this adventure. This is only Book 2, but already the Mont Blanc Rescue team feels like family to me.

Thanks to my beta readers, for always being there to read my work, and for helping me make every book better.

Thanks to my ARC readers, for dropping everything to read the book and giving me your honest feedback.

To my editor—thank you for working your magic on my stories. As always, any errors remaining are my own.

Thanks to Maria Spada, from *Maria Spada Book Cover Design*, for the beautiful cover.

Made in the USA
Las Vegas, NV
09 January 2023

65321064R00157